# THE WILD WAY HOME

## SOPHIE KIRTLEY

BLOOMSBURY
CHILDREN'S BOOKS

LONDON  OXFORD  NEW YORK  NEW DELHI  SYDNEY

BLOOMSBURY CHILDREN'S BOOKS
Bloomsbury Publishing Plc
50 Bedford Square, London WC1B 3DP, UK

BLOOMSBURY, BLOOMSBURY CHILDREN'S BOOKS and the
Diana logo are trademarks of Bloomsbury Publishing Plc

First published in Great Britain in 2020 by Bloomsbury Publishing Plc

A catalogue record for this book is available from the British Library

ISBN: PB: 978-1-5266-1628-9; eBook: 978-1-5266-1627-2

8 10 9 7

Typeset by RefineCatch Limited, Bungay, Suffolk

Printed and bound in Great Britain by CPI Group (UK) Ltd, Croydon CR0 4YY

To find out more about our authors and books visit www.bloomsbury.com and
sign up for our newsletters

*For my pack:*
*Lyla, Arlo, Flora,*
*Andrew.*
*With love.*
*xxx*
*xXx*

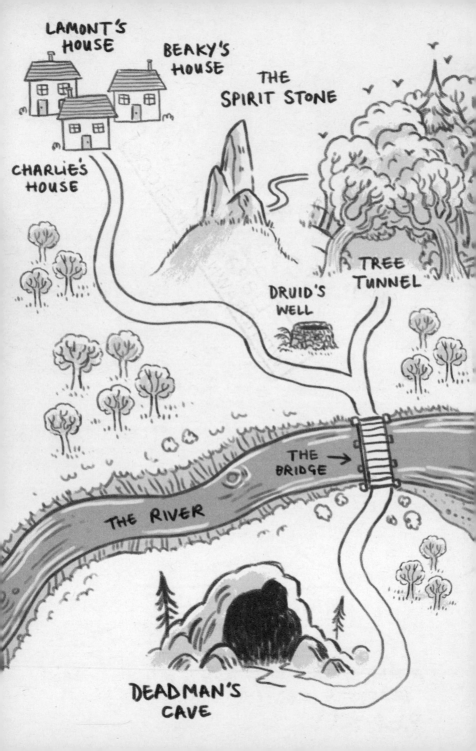

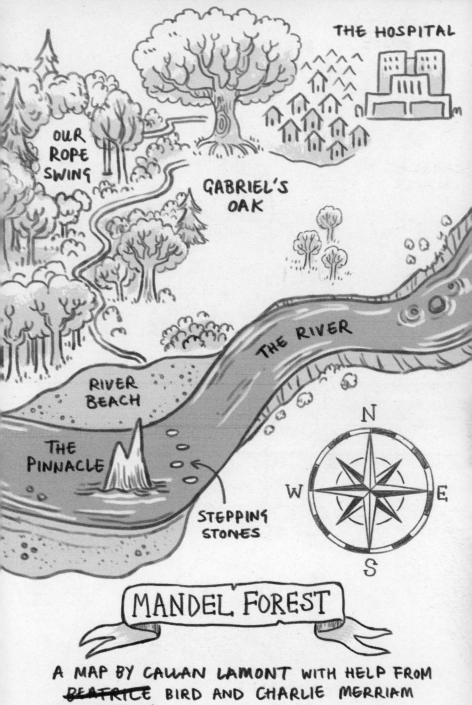

*I went out to the hazel wood,*
*Because a fire was in my head,*
*And cut and peeled a hazel wand,*
*And hooked a berry to a thread;*
*And when white moths were on the wing,*
*And moth-like stars were flickering out,*
*I dropped the berry in a stream*
*And caught a little silver trout.*

*When I had laid it on the floor*
*I went to blow the fire a-flame,*
*But something rustled on the floor,*
*And someone called me by my name*

W.B. Yeats, 'The Song of Wandering Aengus'

*BEFORE ...*

Early on midsummer's morning, as the first blackbird sang and as the last white moth fluttered away, a baby was born in a clearing amidst the trees.

The first creature this baby saw was a hart with magnificent antlers. The baby looked at the hart and the hart looked at the baby and for a tiny moment all was still in the endless forest.

So Ma gave thanks to the hart and named her baby Hartboy, because all this happened 6,000 years ago, and it was just how things were done.

From that morning onwards, Hartboy, like all his people, wore a deertooth threaded on his necklet; the deertooth made him safe. Seasons came and went; leaves sprouted and fell; Hartboy learned and grew. With each midsummer

*Ma carved a fresh line on to Hartboy's deertooth to mark the passing of his time.*

*Then one midsummer, when there were twelve lines in all, Hartboy's deertooth was lost ...*

AFTER...

# HUNT

I hide on the mossy branch of the hazel tree, my legs dangling into nothing. I wait. The wind rustles the leaves; a wood pigeon coos; the forest creaks and cracks like old bones.

A wordless shout. From the direction of Deadman's Cave. The Hunters are coming.

I squint into the hazy sunlight; I can see a ripple of trembling trees where they carve and smash through the forest. The crack-thump-rip of sticks grows louder as they tear their way closer and closer to my hiding place.

The Hunters hack through the bracken and out into the patch of sunshine, right at the foot of my tree.

It's them.

Lamont. Beaky. Nero.

I don't dare breathe.

Lamont stands, hand on hip, and peers into the forest. Beaky circles the tree, jabbing at rabbit holes, prodding the undergrowth with a long, sharp stick. Nero growls, black ears pricked, hackles raised, nose to the ground.

My heart thuds hard and loud.

Nero stops. He sniffs and lifts his nose towards me.

Then Nero turns his head sharply away. He can hear something, something else. Then I hear it too: there's rustling in the bracken.

Nero looks to Lamont. Lamont lifts a finger to his thin lips. Beaky nods.

They think the noise is me.

The thing in the undergrowth rustles again.

Lamont signals a countdown with his fingers:

*Three.*

*Two.*

*One.*

The Hunters charge into the bushes, yelling, their sticks raised high.

A young deer bounds out on the opposite side, tail pale amongst the tree shadows. It springs away and is gone.

Nero chases after the deer, barking.

'NERO!' yell Lamont and Beaky, waist-deep in a tangle of brambles.

I see my chance.

I touch wood, just for luck, then I scramble from my tree and I run.

Beaky shouts, 'It's Charlie!'

But I don't look back. Down the hill, through the forest, towards the river. My feet pound the ground and my fists pummel the air. I charge over the wooden bridge, and up the steep gravel path on the other side. Each breath is heavy. My chest hurts. At Druid's Well, I swerve off the path and run straight up through the bracken. I know exactly where I'm going.

I hear the thump of the Hunters running across the bridge. They're gaining on me.

I pass the rope swing and run through the patch of wild mint until I reach the edge of the clearing. Panting, I look back over my shoulder: all clear. I run out of the tree cover and up the mound, tugging on tufts of grass to heave myself right up to the top.

I reach the Spirit Stone and I lean with my forehead pressed on to the cool grey rock.

'Home!' I say, high-fiving the Spirit Stone.

Slumping down on to the grass, I close my eyes and gasp air into my aching lungs.

I won the game.

Nero reaches the Spirit Stone next. He just stands there panting. Lamont and Beaky don't bother running the last bit, not once they know I've beaten them. Lamont clambers up the mound and flops down next to me.

'Close one, Charlie,' he says. 'That deer put us off.'

'Just you blame the deer,' I say. Lamont does a little half-laugh and pokes me in the side. Nero comes over, long tail wagging, his eyes on the stick in his owner's hand.

'Go get it, Nero.' Lamont tosses the stick into the clearing. Nero charges all the way back down the hill again.

'Oi!' yells Beaky, still staggering up the mound. 'You nearly got me with that stick, Lamont!' When Beaky finally reaches the Spirit Stone she collapses beside us, breathing hard. 'Next time,' she pants, 'there's absolutely – no – way – I'm being – a Hunter – that forest is far – far –' she swallows – 'far too big – to find – anyone – in.'

'Just you blame the forest, Beaky,' I say. We all laugh, even Beaky.

We sit there, saying nothing, gazing out over our forest. I look at the gleaming river; I follow its twists and bends all the way through the forest, right out to where it widens and becomes the distant silver haze of the sea. I look at the far-off farmland cut neatly into green rectangles of fields, like slices of cake. I look at the town, how it spreads greyly up from the riverbanks, surrounding our forest, which surrounds this clearing, which surrounds this mound, which surrounds the Spirit Stone. *Home.* If I stretch my neck, I can just about see the roof of my actual home, where Dad is probably making tea for poor Mum, still stuck in bed waiting for the baby who'll be born soon.

## STONES

The baby was supposed to come three days ago. 'D-Day,' Dad called it.

Mum's been counting the days off on the kitchen calendar with a big red pen; she's not been well so the doctors put her on 'bed rest' last month and it's driving her absolutely bananas. I breathe in the warm summer air, watching a flock of noisy swifts flit and swoop in the clear blue sky. I wouldn't be able to stand it either, being stuck inside in summer, not able to do anything fun at all. It'll be worth it in the end though. A little tingle creeps up my spine; soon I'll have a brother or a sister, and everything will change.

The light has that golden tinge now and the shadows are stretched. I take a smooth pebble out of my pocket.

Squinting up at the Spirit Stone, I move the pebble back and forward in the air, taking aim at the Spirit Stone's pointy peak.

Beaky sits up on her elbows to watch. I fling the pebble; it arcs up and over the Spirit Stone.

'Missed!' calls Beaky, flopping back down.

'Don't eat stones, Nero!' shouts Lamont as his dog charges off to find the pebble. Seconds later Nero's back, crunching away.

'Wow! He really listens to you, Lamont,' I say, in fake admiration.

'Shut up,' says Lamont, wheedling the pebble out from Nero's jaws. 'Do you want this back? Maybe add it to your collection?'

I laugh. 'No thanks. You can keep it, Lamont.'

'It's not just a *collection*, it's *Mandel Museum*!' says Beaky in a posh voice.

'I haven't called it that since we were in Year Two, Beaky!' I protest, laughing.

She ignores me. 'And that slobbery old stone's not quite weird enough. What's it going to look like next to the badger skull, and the arrowhead and the bird's nest, and the ...' Beaky lies there and lists all the things I've collected from the forest since we were little. Her eyes are shut and her long red hair is spread out on the grass. Lamont balances Nero's wet pebble on her forehead. Beaky shuts up, sits up and thumps him. I laugh again.

The evening sun is warm on my face. Shutting my eyes, I stroke Nero's silky soft ears. I sigh. I really ought to go home. Check on Mum. See if I've got a brother yet … or a sister.

'I'm off,' I say, standing up. 'See you tomorrow.'

'… for your birrrthdaaay!' sings Beaky. 'I can't wait! D'you think you'll finally get a phone, Charlie?'

'Maybe,' I say, crossing my fingers behind my back.

'Are we still camping out tomorrow night?' asks Lamont.

'Of course we are,' answers Beaky, before I even have a chance to think about it. Nero wags his tail like he's in agreement.

I pat Nero's black head. 'I guess it depends on the baby.' My shrug turns into a little shiver of excitement.

'Maybe baby!' grins Beaky, nudging me in the ribs.

I grin back. 'I'd better go.' I scramble to my feet. 'Bye!' I yell over my shoulder as I turn and run back down through the clearing and on to the gravel path through the forest.

Among the trees the air tastes cool and shadowy. The

branches on either side of the path lean in slightly, so it's dark like a tunnel. I can still hear the faint echo of Lamont and Beaky's laughter. A big clumsy bird flaps out of a tree, so close to my head I duck. My foot skids out in front of me and I end up sitting on the path. The bird lands on a branch, beady eyes staring at me. It's a wood pigeon with feathers the colours of early morning sky: grey and pink and silver.

I look down at the gravel I disturbed when I slipped. One small, pale stone catches my eye. I pick it up and rub it on my shorts to clean it. It's whitish, smooth, about the size and shape of an almond. I stare at the dull gleam of the stone on my muddy palm, and I realise it's not a stone at all. It's a tooth! A little shiver tingles like a breath across my shoulder blades.

A tooth, root and all! Wow! And it's not small either, must be from quite a decent-sized animal – a badger? A fox maybe? Or a deer? I don't care if Beaky and Lamont tease me about it; this tooth is definitely going in my collection. I've never found a tooth in Mandel Forest before. I get to my feet, pressing the tooth's pointy end into my fingertip; it leaves a little dimple there. I slide it into my pocket.

I feel the weight of someone watching me.

'Lamont? Beaky?' I call. It would be just like them to sneak up on me, get revenge for not winning the game.

There's no one here.

The wood pigeon in the tree ruffles his feathers noisily and I nearly jump out of my skin. 'You scared me!' I say as I gaze up at him. His feathers shimmer, swirling colours of oil on water.

The wood pigeon stares back. 'Whooo?' he says, his head cocked to one side. 'Whooooo? Whooooooooooo?'

I laugh.

'I'm Charlie Merriam,' I reply, and the wood pigeon flaps off.

**Chollie. Murr. Umm,** says a low voice from high in the tree behind me. A human voice. A voice I do not know.

I run. Faster than I've ever run before. Because this time it's not a game.

# HOME

The forest is a blur of green and the only sound I can hear is the pounding of my heart. I reach the fork, then I sprint up the path and along past the high wooden fences, to my gate, to my garden, to home.

I burst in the back door.

'Mum!' I yell.

'What's the matter with you, Charlie?' asks Dad. He's cooking spaghetti in the kitchen.

I can't even speak I'm so out of breath.

Mum shuffles to the doorway in her dressing gown. She looks really tired even though she's been in bed for weeks.

'Are you OK, love?' she asks.

I try to work out in my head how to explain to them

what just happened. I always tell Mum and Dad everything, even the bad stuff, even the scary stuff, even the silly stuff. I open my mouth to tell them about the voice I heard in the woods. Then I realise how utterly ridiculous and stupid it sounds; they'll just say my imagination's running away again. I close my mouth, because even if they *did* believe me they'd only worry and then they'd probably cancel my birthday camping.

'Charlie?' Dad already sounds worried.

'I'm fine,' I finally answer.

'O ... K ... ' says Mum, drawing out each syllable and raising one eyebrow.

'I'm fine,' I say again with a pretend smile, remembering last summer when I told my mum about the leech Beaky thought she saw in the river and we all got banned from swimming right through the holidays.

'Are *you* OK?' I pant at her. 'No baby yet?'

Mum puts her hand on her utterly massive belly and rolls her eyes. 'Not quite yet,' she says. Dad laughs. Mum doesn't.

She looks me up and down, then shakes her head wearily. 'Charlie Merriam, you are absolutely filthy! What have you been doing in that forest?'

'Sorry, Mum,' I say, knowing she doesn't really want

an answer. I wash my hands and glance at the black-and-white baby scan stuck to the fridge. The baby looks like a little alien, its head almost the same size as its body, its arms and legs so small and wheedly they look more shrimp-ish than human.

'Hello, Little Big-Head!' I whisper to the picture, like I always do.

'Dinner's ready!' says Dad.

Mum lowers herself into the chair and sighs at me.

'Always late and always filthy,' she grumbles.

'That's Charlie's motto, don't you know?' says Dad chirpily as he brings the bowls of spag bol over to the table.

'Wild thing!' he chuckles, ruffling my hair.

A smile flickers across Mum's face.

'We used to call you that when you were little, Charlie.'

'I know, I remember,' I say, smiling back.

'Some things never change,' says Dad, twirling up a forkful of spaghetti. Over his shoulder I stare at the scan of the alien baby, curled up like a prawn, waiting in the dark, getting ready to be born.

I slurp up a worm of spaghetti, licking the sauce from my lips. For as long as I can remember I've wished for a brother or a sister, and now my wish is nearly really actually about to come true. Excitement flutters in my chest and I grin so wide I can feel my ears hum.

'Maybe lateness runs in the family,' I say, nodding at Mum's belly. And even Mum laughs this time.

I kneel on my bed and look out of the window. Even though it's almost bedtime the sky is still pale blue; the moon, round as a coin, glows silver in the half-light. Downstairs I can hear the TV mumbling away and the rise and fall of Mum and Dad's voices.

Next to me on my bed is the battered black tin chest where I keep my collection. On the lid is a grubby old bit of masking tape; written on it is *Mandel Museum*, in my clumsy writing from before I could even do joined-up. I pull off the tape and squish it up into a little ball. I open the lid. It used to be Dad's fishing box and the inside is divided up into loads of different sections, and each little section contains something I've found in the forest. There's so much stuff that sometimes even *I'm* surprised at what I've got in here. I peer at the owl pellet full of tiny bones; the green glass fragment washed smooth by the river; the four-leaf clover, folded in Sellotape for protection; the sharpened flint microlith; the curled-up scrolls of papery birch bark.

I reach into my pocket and set the tooth carefully on my window sill; it gleams dully in the fading light. Then I pick up the book that's always next to my bed; it's called *The Wild* and it's my favourite book. I won it in a raffle at school, before I could even read. Back then I just liked the pictures: the amber-eyed lynx on the prowl, who looked like a bigger, more dangerous, more exciting version of our cat, Howard Carter; the dragonfly nymphs, like giant earwigs with their horrible pincers; the bats ... when I was little I always used to turn the book the wrong way up when I got to the bats page so that I could look properly at the roosting pipistrelles.

Downstairs the TV audience does a big laugh and I hear Mum and Dad's laughter like icing on top of it. I flick to the index and run my finger down the columns of words, pausing at any possibles, hoping I'll find the once-upon-a-time owner of that tooth.

*Badger* ...

*Bear* ...

*Bison* ...

*Deer* ... I read and I flick through to page 245. And there's the photo of the fisherman who's gripping the antlers of a massive ancient deer skull that he's just pulled out of a lake. I pick up the real-life tooth and hold it close to the picture, trying to compare it. A breeze drifts in through the open window, ruffling the pages. 'Deer tooth?' I whisper, pressing down on the tooth's tip.

Then, from somewhere else, somewhere outside, I hear that low gravelly voice again. Cholliemurrum, almost like it's saying my name.

I freeze, staring out of the window into the stillness of the garden and the dim of Mandel Forest beyond.

'Who's there?' I squeak.

But nobody answers.

Of course not.

I *am* just imagining stuff.

The summer breeze swishes the leaves. It's only the wind. Only the wind.

'Charlieeee!'

My heart lurches but it's just Dad calling up the stairs. I laugh at myself then.

'Charlie Merriam! Stop reading and turn that light out – it's late and you've got a big day tomorrow!'

'OK, Dad!' I slip the deertooth back into my shorts pocket, pack my collection away and start to get ready for bed. Tomorrow will be here soon, and tomorrow's my twelfth birthday!

# BIRTHDAYS

'Charlie,' whispers Dad, 'Charlie, wake up.'

I roll over and open my eyes. It's still dark. Dad's crouched down by my bed; his face looks pale in the moonlight. My clock says 03.03. Not even morning! I close my eyes again.

'Charlie!' This time I hear the urgency in his voice. 'Charlie Merriam!'

Something's wrong. I sit straight up.

'Is Mum OK? Is the baby coming?'

'The baby's here, Charlie! We had to dash off to hospital in the night; we didn't want to wake you up so Margot from next door came over.' Dad grins the biggest, cheesiest grin. 'Charlie, you've got a little brother!'

I smile back. A baby! A baby brother!

Then I stop smiling and go all cold inside.

'Mum?'

'Don't worry, love, Mum's fine. Women have been having babies since the beginning of time. She's just very tired and a bit … surprised – the baby came much faster than you did when you were born.' Dad reaches out and strokes my hair.

I smile again and at the same time my eyes fill up with tears.

'Why're you crying, you big banana?' Dad cuddles me. His chin is prickly and his breath smells of coffee, but I cuddle him back.

'I'm not crying.' I sniff.

Dad kisses the top of my head.

'Hang on a minute.' He gets up and darts out of my room. I hear him galloping down the stairs.

I can't believe the baby's been born.

Today.

I kneel on my bed and look through the open window at the full moon; it's all blurry because of the tears. I rub my eyes and take a deep breath of cool night air.

Today is *my* birthday.

Just thinking it makes my eyes well up again. Why am I even crying? It's my birthday! And I've got … a brother … the one thing I've always wished for. That's way more important than having a birthday all to yourself.

'You're a nutball, Charlie Merriam,' I say to myself through my stupid tears.

Outside a blackbird starts to sing. Another bird joins in and another and another until the whole dark garden and the whole dark forest beyond are alive with birdsong. I try to stop myself from crying by thinking about birds, not babies.

*Birds don't have birthdays. They only live for a few years and then they die.*

Then I'm thinking about dead birds, and that doesn't exactly cheer me up.

The photo in the silver frame by my bed catches my eye. It's the one of Mum and Dad and me from when *I* was just born. Twelve years ago today. I lift the photo into the moonlight so that I can see us properly. Mum and Dad look kind of the same, just a bit less old and a bit less chubby. But it's hard to believe that I was that baby; that baby is actually me.

But now there's another baby. A new one. The hot tears rise again.

I hear Dad galumphing back upstairs.

'Happy birthday to you.' He comes round my door, singing, his face lit up with candlelight. 'Happy birthday to you.'

In one hand Dad is holding one of Mum's scented candles from the mantelpiece so the air smells of waxy jasmine blossom; on his other hand he's balancing a Mr Kipling French Fancy. He's kind of got it all wrong and kind of got it all right at the same time. I giggle and wipe my eyes on the corner of my covers.

'Happy birthday, dear Charlieeeeeee.' He smiles so wide when he sings the end of my name. 'Happy birthday to yoooooooooo!' he hoots.

My lips make the blowing shape and I shut my eyes to make the same secret wish I've always wished. But then I have to open them again because I can't wish my old wish any more. For as long as I can remember, I've wished that I could stop being an only child. And now ...

I grin at Dad. 'A brother!' I say. 'My brother!' The words feel all new and strange in my mouth.

'Yep.' Dad grins back. He looks all dazed, like he doesn't quite believe it either.

So I close my eyes and blow out my candle.

Dad bows grandly and presents me with the yellow French Fancy.

'Thanks.' I take it and bite off the creamy top bit. 'The lemon ones are my favourites.'

'I know. Mine too.' Dad produces another, slightly dented, French Fancy from his jacket pocket. 'Cheers!' We clink our French Fancies together and Dad sits down on my bed.

We munch and listen to the skyful of birdsong. It's just starting to get light.

'Your brother wasn't born today, you know,' says Dad, staring out of the window. 'Eleven thirty-two last night in fact.' Dad puts his arm around me. 'So you can have your birthday back.'

'Thanks.' I look up at him and he gives my shoulder a squeeze; Dad looks tired and happy and crumby. The little balloon of happiness in my chest starts to puff back up again. 'What's the baby called?'

'Dara.'

'Dara.' My new brother's name sounds soft and wispy when I say it; I try it again, this time in a strong voice. 'Dara!' Now he sounds like a warrior. 'Dara. OK.'

I lean into Dad's hug even though I'm twelve now and probably getting too old for so much soppy cuddling. Then Dad starts to hum quietly; I recognise the tune right away and I sigh: it's the first song I ever knew – the silly song Dad always used to sing to me at bedtime when I was little. I know what's coming, but for some reason I don't tell Dad to be quiet. Sure enough, Dad starts to sway gently, then soft-as-soft he sings:

'Row, row, row your boat

Off into the night

And if you meet a tiger

Don't give him a fright ...

... Raaaaaaaaa!' Dad growls in my ear, trying to make me jump.

I just giggle. I remember how he always used to change the animal every bedtime so I never quite knew which one we'd *meet*. I shake my head at him, still laughing. 'You're such a nutball, Dad!'

Dad pretends to be offended. 'Don't know what you think is so funny, Charlie Merriam. It's a very serious life lesson; ah well, you'll thank me one day ... should you ever find yourself in tiger country, that is ...'

'Oh, Dad!' I say, and I snuggle in. Just for a moment I let myself feel little again, little and loved and safe.

We sit together and listen to the singing of the birds in the wide-awake forest. Dad yawns a big long yawn. I gaze out of my window; in the last of the bluey dark a tiny moth flutters up, up and is gone. She's heading for the moon.

## BABY

'Dad,' I whisper, 'Dad! Wake up!'

Midsummer sunshine is pouring through my window. We must've both fallen asleep. I can hear Dad's phone vibrating like an angry hornet.

I wriggle out from under Dad's sleep-heavy arm and give him a good shake.

'Dad! Come on! Where's your phone? It's probably Mum!'

'Mum?!' he says, sitting suddenly upright, like someone has just pressed his on switch. 'Where's Mum?'

'Where do you think she is?' I say, rolling my eyes at him. 'In hospital with Dara maybe?'

The phone (wherever it is) stops buzzing.

'Oh yes,' says Dad, sinking back again, a big dozy

grin on his face. 'Dara Merriam, I almost forgot about that one.'

His phone starts vibrating again.

'Where have you put your stupid phone, Dad?'

'In my shoe,' says Dad as if that is the most obvious answer in the world; as if that's where every sensible adult keeps their phone. I raise an eyebrow at him and reach under my bed, grabbing the shoe, which I hand to Dad.

'Thanks,' he says, and pretends that the shoe itself is the phone. 'Hello?'

I can't help laughing even though he is being totally ridiculous. He finally answers it properly.

'Hello, love,' he says to Mum. 'Sorry. Couldn't find my phone.'

I shake my head at him. Over at the hospital, I imagine, Mum is probably shaking her head at him too.

'I know. Sorry. How are you? How's Dara? ... Great, that's great ... Charlie? Yeah, Charlie's grand.' Dad winks at me. 'No, of course I didn't forget; we had birthday cake at three in the morning! Yes ... with candles.'

I laugh. Holding up my index finger, I mouth the words, 'One candle!'

'Yep. Right beside me. Yep, 'course you can. Here's Charlie.'

I take the phone. 'Hi, Mum.'

Mum sings 'Happy Birthday to You' very quietly, like it's a big secret. I imagine she doesn't want to wake the baby.

'Thanks, Mum,' I say. 'How're you?'

'I'm fine, thanks, Charlie. Here, listen, your brother wants to say something to you.'

I listen to the shuffling sound as Mum puts the phone next to Dara. Then nothing. Or maybe the tiniest whisper of his breath.

Then Mum's voice comes back on. 'Did you catch that?' she asks softly. 'He just wanted to wish you a happy birthday.'

'Thanks, Mum.' I smile. 'Tell him happy birthday from me too.'

Mum laughs. Even her laugh sounds smaller and quieter than usual. 'Love you, Charlie. Can't wait to see you in a bit.'

'Love you too, Mum. See you later. Bye.' I pass the phone back to Dad.

'Hello again, so when are they releasing you from captivity? ... Right.' Dad gets up and wanders out of my room. 'When will that be?'

I lean my elbows on the window sill and look outside.

It's a beautiful day; the air tastes warm and full of promise. I love it that our house is right on the edge of Mandel Forest; you just open the gate at the bottom of our garden and you're there – in the oldest wood in the whole country. I can smell the sweet scent of honeysuckle and the sharp stink of elderflower; the leaves of the birch trees at the forest's edge flicker silver in the sunlight. I stand up on the window sill; over the hill on the other side of the forest I can just see the glinting metal roof of the hospital tower – that's where Mum is. I smile to myself. And Dara. In one of the neighbours' gardens a lawnmower engine hums; somewhere else little kids are playing. I can hear them squealing and squeaking like kittens. I lean out a bit so I can see into Lamont's garden, just in case he's there. But there's only Nero, snoozing in the morning sun.

'Lamont!' I yell. 'Hey, Lamont!'

I hear the clunk and slide of his bedroom window opening, then his tousled head appears.

'Hi, Charlie.' Lamont yawns. 'Happy birthday!'

That takes me by surprise a bit because I'd almost forgotten. I can't believe I'd almost forgotten my own birthday!

'Thanks.' I say. 'Guess what?'

'You got a phone?'

'Nope. Not yet anyway. I got a brother!'

Lamont's eyes widen like he's suddenly awake and he grins a huge grin. 'Wooooohooooo!' he yells. 'That's brilliant, Charlie! A brother! I'm jealous!'

Lamont has one sister, Marie. She's fourteen and she's only interested in horses and boyfriends.

'A brother!' he says again. 'What's his name?'

'Dara,' I say. The word feels very new when I say it.

'Nice,' says Lamont.

'Nice,' I say back, and we grin at each other out of our bedroom windows.

I hear Lamont's mum calling him from inside the house.

'Gotta go,' he says, and his head disappears back through his window. Then pops straight back out, like a cuckoo in a cuckoo clock.

'Brilliant!' he says, and he gives me a big thumbs up before he vanishes inside again.

I smile proudly to myself, all tingly and warm inside, because Lamont's right, it *is* brilliant to have a brother at last. 'I'm the eldest,' I say to myself, practising. I look at my tatty old playhouse, abandoned for years at the bottom of the garden. I'll paint it up again really nicely, blue and white. I'll fill my old sandpit with new sand too

31

and Dara can play in it when he's bigger. I imagine taking Dara paddling in the river for the first time, when he can walk of course. Then I imagine holding his hand as he toddles along the high street and, in my head, Mrs Rodriguez, my old primary school teacher, comes out of the Co-op and sees us.

*Who's this then, Charlie?* she asks in my daydream.

'This is my little brother, Dara,' I say out loud, bringing myself back to where I actually am.

I hear a real-life miaow. It's Howard Carter, my cat, who's in the kitchen, still waiting for his breakfast. Poor old Howard Carter! Usually Mum feeds him first thing, or Dad. Maybe looking after Howard Carter will end up being my job now that Dara's here. I head downstairs to feed him.

As I pass Mum and Dad's bedroom I hear Dad's voice from behind the closed door.

'Are you sure?' He sounds serious.

I stop to listen.

'Are you sure you're sure? Did you mention it to the doctor?'

My heart starts to thud.

'OK. OK, love. Calm down. We'll be in to see you later. It's all right ... It's all right.'

*Is something wrong with Mum? With the baby?*

'No, no, of course I won't say anything to Charlie … Yep. Yep. Will do. Give Dara a kiss from me too. Love you. Bye.'

Dad opens the door and nearly bowls me over.

'Oh,' he says.

'What exactly *won't you say to Charlie?*'

'Oh,' he says again.

'What's wrong? Is Mum sick? Is Dara all right?'

'No. Mum's not sick, Charlie. She's just a bit tired and upset because it's been a long day and a long night. She wants to come home, with Dara, so we can all be together.'

'Well, why can't they come home?'

'They will. The doctors just need to check them both over and say it's OK first.'

'Then why's Mum so worried?'

Dad hesitates. 'She's not worried.'

My dad is a really bad liar. I stare at him until his eyes meet mine.

'Charlie.' He sighs again. 'We don't want *you* to worry …'

'Dad!' I sigh back at him. 'I'm already worried! And I'd rather know what to worry about, otherwise I'll

33

just worry anyway. I'll worry about stuff that isn't even actually happening.'

Dad thinks about that for a minute and finally nods.

'And I'm twelve now anyway. I can handle it.'

Dad smiles; his eyes crinkle up at the edges.

'Mum's a bit worried about Dara. The doctors did some tests. They listened to Dara's heart and it doesn't sound quite right. So they're doing some scans and things, to check that everything's fine. That's all. It's probably nothing. Nothing to worry about.' Dad smiles at me but this time it doesn't reach his eyes.

I nod and give Dad a little smile back.

'OK,' I say. Behind my back I cross my fingers so tight it hurts, as my head whirls with thoughts about my new baby brother and his tiny not-right heart.

# DARA

I see Mum through the glass door before she sees me. She's sitting up in the hospital bed with the covers over her legs, staring out of the big window. Usually Mum ties her hair back but today it's big and frizzy and wild.

We open the door. Mum turns to face us. She smiles and stretches out her hand to me.

'Charlie!' she says. 'Happy birthday!'

'Hi, Mum.'

Mum takes my hand and squeezes it. 'It's great to see you, Charlie.'

Her hand feels too hot. I squeeze it back, then I shove my hand into my pocket.

'Great to see you too.'

I don't want to meet Mum's eyes, in case I see a sadness there that I don't want to be true.

I look around the room: a metal bed with Mum in it; a red chair with Dad on it; a folded-away TV screen; a small white cupboard; dangly medical stuff attached to the wall.

'Where's the baby?' I ask quietly. My neck prickles with a horrible cold, worried feeling.

'Dara's ...' Mum starts to answer, but then the door opens and a nurse bustles in backwards pulling a squeaky trolley, with a transparent baby bed on top, a bit like a fish tank.

'Here's little one!' says the nurse brightly.

I stand back to let the nurse park the trolley next to Mum's bed.

'Beautiful little brother you've got there, love,' she says to me with a smile.

She writes something on a clipboard and goes out again.

'Come here, Charlie,' says Dad. But he's not looking at me, he's gazing into the baby bed and his eyes have gone all melty. Mum's staring dreamily at the baby too.

A little pang of jealousy wriggles in my tummy. Trying to smile, I squish the pang away, step closer to the baby bed and peer in.

Dara.

My brother.

Maybe it sounds daft, but I'd thought I'd kind of recognise him, just see immediately that he's my brother, but ... he looks not like I expected at all. I think of all those wriggly, giggly babies you see in nappy adverts and I swallow. Dara doesn't look like that.

I stare down at him:

He's so small, so impossibly small, and his face is kind of squashed-looking and weirdly wrinkly, like his skin is too big for him. He's really still as well; just lying there, asleep, his hands up next to his head, tiny fists curled tight. Only his chest moves, rising and falling very quickly as he breathes. It makes me nervous, his too-fast breath.

Mum and Dad are watching me. 'He's beautiful,' I say. I smile at them, but I look away again fast, before they spot that my smile is pretend. I feel so bad about it but I don't think that my new brother actually *is* beautiful at all.

The honest truth is that Dara frightens me; everything I notice about him is kind of ... not right. His skin is grey, not pink like it should be; his lips are in a tiny O shape like he's whistling but I think they're slightly blue. What scares me the most though is that he has a very thin tube, like a straw from an apple-juice carton, going right round his head and into his nose.

Dara.

I blink down at the disappointment of him, still smiling my pretend smile, and also trying not to cry. He suddenly scrunches up his face; the surprise of his movement makes me jump and Dad laughs at me.

'Don't worry, Charlie, he won't bite,' smiles Dad, rubbing my shoulder. I shake him off, I don't know why, and Dad looks a bit hurt.

'Why don't you sit down, Charlie, and you can give your brother a cuddle,' says Mum.

As if he hates the idea too, the baby starts to cry. I stare into his toothless little mouth and I realise what he reminds me of: Dara's like a baby bird, just hatched, before it has feathers or fluff or open eyes. I shudder, then check quickly to see if Mum and Dad have noticed my reaction, but they're not looking at me now. They're too busy soothing the baby. His cry fills the room, a horrible, thin squawk, birdlike too. I want to cover my ears, but I know that's babyish, not the right thing to do at all, so I just bite hard on my lip and look out the window; we're high up in the hospital tower and all I see is blue.

'Sit down then,' says Dad to me, a bit impatient. He's holding the baby, who looks smaller than ever in Dad's big arms. So small. So fragile. Dara stops crying and opens his eyes – they're dark and starey.

'Can he see?' I ask as I sit on the red chair. Neither Mum nor Dad answer me, they're both trying to sort out the nose tube and the little plastic thing in Dara's hand, which has a tube as well. The red chair plastic pinches my bare legs as I wriggle. I pull at my shorts, trying to get comfy.

Dara starts crying again. The noise makes me feel all hot and bothered.

'Time for a cuddle with Charlie – that'll cheer you up,' says Dad to the baby.

I feel a bit panicky. What if it doesn't cheer him up? 'Hang on, Dad …' I mumble, but Dad's not listening to me, he's listening to Mum, who's fussing about, trying to find Dad's phone to take a picture, but Dad's lost it as usual and Dara's crying harder than ever and then he stops crying really suddenly with a little gulp and I notice a big cloud of worry cross Dad's face and he and Mum both go utterly quiet and freeze.

I know what they're thinking, because I'm thinking it too: Has the baby stopped breathing? Is he OK?

Dara cries again and they smile at each other, relieved. They don't smile at me.

I just sit on the horrible, pinchy red chair and I feel so invisible it makes me sad, then it makes me cross. Suddenly I want to scream at them. 'I'm here too, you know! I was scared too, you know!'

But I don't scream, I just glare at them, all my jumbled feelings swirling about inside me. They don't notice. Mum's getting the phone ready to take a picture. Dad gets the crying baby ready to have his first cuddle with me. And as Dad lowers Dara towards my arms, something just snaps in me.

'No!' I say. It comes out louder than I mean it to. And I stand up too fast, nearly knocking Dara out of Dad's arms.

'Charlie! What are you doing?' says Mum, shocked. She drops the phone, and it clatters on to the hard floor and flashes, taking a picture of nothing, all by itself. I start to back away from them, towards the door.

At that exact moment the door swings open again. But this time it's not the friendly nurse, it's the doctor. And she's not smiling.

# RESULTS

'Sorry,' I mumble, getting out of the doctor's way.

She gives me a little nod, then she comes in properly, picking up Dad's phone from the floor and handing it to Mum. She stands at the foot of Mum's bed.

'Good afternoon, Mrs Merriam, Mr Merriam,' she says. She has an accent that makes the 'r's in our name sound kind of purr-ish. I look at the cardboard folder in her hand; the results of Dara's tests and scans will be in there.

The doctor taps her pen on the folder; her eyes dart lizard-like from Mum to Dad to Dara to me and back to Dad again.

'Might be best for your eldest to go and ... have a little play, while we have our chat.' She clicks her pen and opens her folder. 'There's a playroom just along the corridor.' She gives me a brisk smile, then her lizard eyes flick to Mum and Dad.

I feel my cheeks going red.

'OK. Yep. No problem,' says Dad to the doctor.

I watch as he so carefully passes Dara to Mum. The baby stops crying almost right away then, like Mum has the magic touch or something. Dara's not asleep though; my brother's starey eyes are still open and he half looks like he's gazing over at me. I stare back at him, feeling cross and sad and sorry and worried all at once.

The lizard doctor click-clicks her pen.

'Charlie?' says Dad. 'Did you hear the doctor, love?'

'I'm going,' I say, my voice all tight and weird.

Mum turns towards me but I don't see what kind of look she's giving me because I'm walking away by now already.

'Hey, Charlie,' says Dad in a really fake-sounding cheerful voice, holding the door for me. 'Here, take this.' He hands me his green canvas backpack. 'There's change in the front pocket – get yourself a drink from the machine. I'll come and find you in a bit.'

I take his stupid backpack and the door shuts itself slowly behind me.

I peep back through the criss-cross glass. Mum sits so still on the bed, like a wild-haired sculpture of herself. Dad nods as he listens to what the doctor says, his eyebrows squeezed close together.

For as long as I can remember I've imagined what it would be like to have a little brother or sister. I'd always thought it would feel like we were all bigger, stronger, just better if there were more of us. Our house would be loud and hectic and mad like Beaky's. But this doesn't feel at all like how I imagined it.

I see the doctor speaking to Mum and Dad; they're each holding one of Dara's tiny hands as he lies sleeping again in Mum's arms.

And I realise Dad's not just *my* dad now. Mum's not just *my* mum. They're Dara's too.

And Dara? I lean back on the cool hospital wall.

Dara's *my* brother. But it doesn't feel like he is mine. Or that I'm his.

I hear a babble of voices in the corridor. A nurse walks past and smiles at me. She's wheeling another baby in a little fish-tank bed. Behind the nurse, hand in hand, is a mum and a dad and a little girl with her hair in two plaits. The girl's wearing a massive badge that says I'M A BIG SISTER, the dad's holding the string of a big blue

IT'S A BOY! balloon. The mum and the dad smile at me too. I don't smile back.

For an angry flash of a second all I want to do is to get a pin and pop that big balloon. Because it doesn't seem fair. Nothing seems fair at all.

They walk off down the corridor and round the corner, their happy chatter fading. I think about their baby and I think about Dara. I think about the folder the doctor was carrying and all the test results inside it.

From behind the door I hear the sudden sound of Mum wailing. It's a horrible animal cry, high and sharp like Mum is shattering into a thousand pieces. It's the scariest sound I've ever heard. It's the sound of something breaking which can never be fixed.

Heart pounding, I turn and run. My trainers squeak on the lino floor of the corridor. I skid as I charge around the corner, catching a glimpse of the empty playroom with its rainbow murals and scattered toys. The lift opposite pings and the heavy doors glide open: it's empty too so I dive inside and bang on the G button. The silver doors seal themselves with a clunk. My tummy lurches as the lift goes down; the mirrored walls reflect me over and over; endless Charlie Merriams. Head swimming, I shut my eyes. Why did Mum make that noise? Did Dara stop breathing right there in her arms? I squeeze my eyes tighter as my own breath catches in my throat. The lift pings, and I rush out of it before the doors are even properly open. I run past the drinks machine and push through the crowded foyer, following the exit arrow, until I burst out of the slidey doors and into the sunlight.

The heat hits me like a force field. I pause, trying to gulp in cool air, but it feels like breathing soup. Next to me is a security guard who looks at me out of the corner of his eye.

'Lovely day!' he says, dabbing his shiny face with a handkerchief.

I look up, trying to position my head so I can't see the hospital building or electricity cables or anything but sky. It's so blue and empty I'm almost dizzy with it. I watch a gull glide noiselessly seawards; on the far horizon I can see a band of cloud gathering. Even though it's baking hot, the air tastes heavy and humid, like a storm might come.

Shielding my eyes, I gaze up Mandel Rise. Beyond the neat houses, right up there at the top is the forest. It ripples and shimmers greenly in the midsummer sun.

The heat and the noise press down on me, and worry twists like a worm in my belly. I look back over my shoulder; I should go back in there.

Then a siren shriek rips through the air as an ambulance swoops into the car park, blue lights whirling. The sound of terrible things – bones sticking out of broken limbs, families being torn apart, tiny hearts stopping. I don't want to see. I don't want to see.

Before I really know my feet are moving I'm over the road, running up Mandel Rise towards the forest.

# GABRIEL'S OAK

I crash into the gate at the top of the hill feeling like my lungs are going to burst, but I can't stop and think yet. I haul myself over and cannon between the picnic tables to the big oak tree that marks the proper start of Mandel Forest.

'Gabriel's Oak,' I spit bitterly. That's Mum and Dad's stupid name for this tree; they named it after a character from Mum's favourite book apparently. Panting, I bang my fist on the rough bark and stare up into the cool green of the canopy.

The sun's heat is like a weight pressing down on me. My heart feels all fluttery and my mind whirs, all I can think of is that noise Mum made, that awful noise. My eyes start to prickle. No. I'm not going to cry.

I blink away the fog in my eyes and scramble up Gabriel's Oak, squirrel-quick and breathless. Up and up and up, until the branches turn too bendy to take my weight, until when I turn to look at it the world seems small beneath me. I perch on a thick branch and rest my head on the trunk; my whole body aches and throbs as my heartbeat settles.

Through the leaves I glimpse the hospital tower. I wonder which window is Mum's window but there are so many it's impossible to tell. They remind me of those close-up pictures of flies' eyes: all those hundreds of tiny compound eyes, each one seeing something the same but ever so slightly different. I imagine each window is an eye, all watching me. It gives me a little guilty shiver, that feeling of being watched. I should …

No. I turn away from the hospital. Leaning my back on the trunk, I draw up my knees and hug them to my chest. Something spikes the top of my leg. I reach into my shorts pocket and take out the deertooth I found yesterday. Yesterday feels so long ago.

I look at the tooth more carefully this time; it has a little hole in it that I didn't even notice before. The hole's full of mud. I hunt about for a thin twig and poke it until it's all clear. I peep at the green leaves and blue sky through the hole. Close up, I can see minuscule markings scratched on to the tooth's surface, a stripy pattern almost. Squinting, I count the tiny lines. There are twelve of them – twelve like me! I bite my lip. It's my birthday and everything's wrong. I bounce the tooth's pointy tip on the fat part of my thumb.

Voices.

Someone's coming.

I shove the deertooth back in my pocket and sit very very still.

I hear the crunch of footsteps approaching through the forest, heading this way; the voices grow louder too. They're voices I know.

'This way, Nero!' calls Lamont. 'Here, Nero!'

'Neeeeerooooo!' yells Beaky.

My heart leaps and I'm just about to yell hello when a hospital window flashes in the sunlight and I realise I'll have to explain about Dara and suddenly it all just seems too tricky to know what to say. So I say nothing. I squeeze my knees tighter to my chest and breathe very lightly.

'One small step for man … one giant leap for mankind,' declares Beaky as she 'spacewalks' into my line of vision. I roll my eyes, because Beaky always makes that same joke. She sits down right beneath me and Lamont plonks himself beside her. I can still hear Nero rustling about in the bushes somewhere.

'Why is it sooooo hot?' asks Beaky.

'Probably something to do with that!' says Lamont, pointing up at the sun.

'You're hilarious, Lamont. This weather'll be perfect for Charlie's birthday camping though, won't it; clear skies, campfire, stars ...'

I can see that Lamont is giving Beaky one of his *looks*.

'What, Lamont? What did I say?'

'Catch yourself on, Beaky! Charlie won't be camping, Charlie probably won't even be birthdaying with us at all. Charlie will probably just be sitting around at home singing "Twinkle, Twinkle, Little Star" and changing nappies and stuff. You know how much Charlie was wanting this baby to come along. We probably won't see Charlie for weeks now ... months ... years ...'

Up in my hiding spot, my stomach drops. It's like they're describing a different Charlie – a Charlie that should've been me.

Beaky picks a blade of long grass and chews on it like a yokel. 'It's only a baby!' she mumbles grumpily.

'You're only a baby,' says Lamont.

Beaky sticks her long grass in Lamont's ear. He leaps

up with a yell and Nero bounds protectively out of the trees, barking.

'Save me, Nero! Beaky's attacking me!' Lamont laughs and so does Beaky.

'I come in peace,' she says, putting her hands up. Nero sees it as an invitation and clambers all over her, licking her face.

I smile and a big part of me aches to come down from this stupid tree and just muck around with my friends like normal. Or maybe they'll even help me, know what I should do ... I'm just about to reveal my hiding place by starting to drop acorns on their heads, when Lamont's phone rings.

His eyebrows crinkle down as he looks at the screen. 'It's Charlie's dad,' he says, and my blood goes cold.

# RUN

'Yes, it's me. Hello,' says Lamont. 'OK … yes … OK … Oh, right … OK …'

'What's going on?' hisses Beaky. Lamont shushes her with his finger.

'Um … that's … um …' Lamont's gone all stuttery like he can't find the words. His eyes are very serious. 'I'm sorry to hear that … Um, how's Charlie?'

I blush and bite my lip. Guilty, embarrassed, worried all at once.

'Err, no … no, not since this morning.'

Lamont covers the phone with his hand and speaks urgently to Beaky. 'You haven't seen Charlie today, have you?' She shakes her head, wide-eyed.

'No, Beaky hasn't either. So … um … what happened … ?'

There's a long pause then. Lamont does a lot of nodding while he listens to my dad. I bury my face in my knees and press my back hard into the knobbly tree bark, willing Gabriel's Oak to just swallow me up.

'OK,' says Lamont finally. 'Well, we're in the forest now, sure. We can look for Charlie in all our usual places if you like ... No ... no problem at all. We'd like to help.'

I peep down at them. Beaky nods wildly, her hand holding on to Nero's collar so tightly I see her white knuckle bones.

'OK then ... OK. I will ... thanks ... bye.'

Lamont hangs up and puts his phone back in his pocket. 'Charlie's run away,' he says.

'What?' says Beaky. 'Why?'

I cover my ears but I can still hear them talking.

'I don't really get it. I think Charlie had a total melt-down and went off in a strop by the sounds of things.'

I jerk my hands from my ears. *A strop!* Suddenly my shame and embarrassment bends into fury. *A strop!* How dare he? I grit my teeth. Lamont doesn't have a clue how I feel.

'But why would Charlie do that?' whispers Beaky. Nero starts whining.

'It's the baby.' Lamont sounds deadly serious. My anger melts as I listen. 'There's something wrong with the baby's heart. He needs an operation.'

'Oh no!' breathes Beaky, clapping her hand over her mouth. 'Poor baby. When?'

'Today. Soon. That's why we need to find Charlie ASAP ... because ...' Lamont's voice fades away to nothing.

In the pit of my stomach an ice-cold ball of sadness and worry swells and grows until my eyes cloud with tears and a tiny little gulpy whimpery noise comes out of my mouth. I clap my hand over my lips but it's too late.

Nero's ears prick. He looks straight up at me.

'So ... where is Charlie?'

Nero's barking at me now, wagging his tail.

'Your guess is as good as mine, Beaky. Shall we try the Spirit Stone?'

Nero starts going bananas.

'Nero? Stop it! What?'

Nero breaks out of Beaky's hold and jumps up on the trunk of Gabriel's Oak, still barking like crazy.

Lamont and Beaky look straight up at me. Then at each other.

'Hi,' I say sheepishly, my voice all croaky. I feel their

eyes on me as I climb back down and land with a thud on the hard ground.

'What were you doing up there, Charlie?' says Beaky. 'Why were you hiding in that tree?'

I shrug. Nothing I say will make any sense to them. My mood is zigzagging about so fast I don't even make sense to me at the moment.

'Did you hear me talking to your dad?' asks Lamont.

I nod, avoiding his eyes.

'I'm sorry to hear about your baby brother,' whispers Beaky. She touches my arm softly. I yank my arm away from her; for some reason her kindness just makes me cross.

'Sorry,' she mumbles.

Nero whines.

'You'd better go back to the hospital, Charlie,' says Lamont.

I stare at him angrily; who's he to tell me what I should or shouldn't do?

Beaky and Lamont look at each other. It's a secret look, like they're suddenly in a gang I'm not part of. The 'Pity Charlie Club'. Now that baby is here everything has changed. Even my friends.

I grit my teeth in rage and turn away. I focus on the

lumpy old tree root I'm kick-kick-kicking with my toe. Shoving my hands in my pockets, I find the deertooth and I squeeze it so hard it proper hurts.

Everything feels wrong here. I want to run and hide as far away as I can from all of it. Thoughts swarm about in my head like bees. Buzzing. Dara. His little lips pale blue. Mum's puffy eyes. The camera flash. Dad's fake smile. The squeak of my feet on the lino. The wall of heat. The ambulance siren. I swallow and squeeze the deertooth harder. What if Dara dies? My thoughts are so muddly they're making me dizzy.

I close my eyes. Beaky and Lamont are talking to me, but I try to block them out, let their voices go blurry and fade. I concentrate on my thumb as I press it on to the sharp tip of the deertooth in my pocket.

Behind me in the forest, something screeches.

I spin around, opening my eyes just in time to duck as a jay dives straight towards me.

I lift my arms to protect my head. The jay shrieks again as he twists mid-air, then swoops fast and low back past me, his wing feathers flashing blue like a beacon.

Too blue.

I look down; there is a tiny bead of too-red blood on my thumb tip. And all around me the colours of the forest are too much themselves: too green, too blue, too red. All shimmering in the heat. I shake my head hard to clear my ears, because all the sounds have gone muffled, like when you're underwater. Then the jay's back; his shriek cuts through the fuzziness and fills my ears.

The sunlight dapples yellow through the trees; I gaze into the leafy greenness and I can just glimpse the jay, diving towards the distant shimmer of the river. I can't resist. I forget everything and take a big breath and run into the coolness of the forest, following the jay.

I run fast. My feet thump thump on the softness of the mud and mulch. My heart quickens. I lift up my arm and I leap to grab at a dangling leaf. I run, Dad's bag bumping softly on my back. In here the air smells damp and mossy; I gulp it in. I reach the turn where the path slopes down. I run faster still. So fast my legs feel like they aren't even mine; so fast I can hear the thud of my own heart. The path bends, twisting down to the water. I leap a tight turn and my foot skids in the mud. But I don't fall. I run faster. Bracken tickles my hands, nettles too, but I'm so quick they don't even get time to sting me. I can hear it now: the sound of the river trickling over the rocks. I race around the last bend and the sun pours into the dell and flashes silver on the water and it looks so cool and beautiful and I'm so so hot and I leap over the long grass and down the ridge and keep running across the sand at the water's edge, running, splashing right into the river.

I stop.

My heart freezes.

There's someone in the river.

Face down.

# WAKE UP!

I don't stop to think. Two steps and I'm there. The body's floating in a rocky pool but the water's slow here and only knee-deep. It's a girl. Her hair's all long and floating on the water. There's blood coming out of her head; it's making red swirls in the clear river. Near her is a jagged rock which is smeared in blood. She must've slipped, bashed her head on the rock.

I grab the girl under the arms and try to lift her. She's so heavy! I heave with all my strength and lift her shoulders clear of the water. Her head dangles down over her chest. I lean right back. Her head flops on to my shoulder and her body turns and my feet slip and I fall so I'm sitting there in the shallow pool with the girl who is lying limp in my arms. I push the wet tangled hair out of her face.

It's not a girl. It's a boy.

His eyes are closed. I hold my wet hand in front of his open mouth. No warm air. He's not breathing. He's not breathing!

I scramble about, trying to find a foothold on the shifting pebbles of the river bed. I grip the wild-haired boy under his arms and I lean and I stumble and I slip as I drag him backwards out of the water. At last we reach the gravelly sand of the beach. I lay him down on his side and collapse to my knees next to him, panting. The boy doesn't move. I look around for someone to help us.

'HELP!' I shout, as loud as I can. 'HELP!'

My voice sounds so small in the tallness of the forest. The only reply is the far-off squawk of a bird, shrill and raw like a baby's cry.

'BEAKY!' I yell. 'LAMONT! Come quick, I need you NOW!'

But they don't answer. No one does.

The boy's lips are blue. I touch his wrist and I don't know if it's true or if it's just what I want to believe, but I think I feel the tiniest flicker of his pulse. He's alive! At least I think he's alive.

'HELP!' I yell so loud my throat hurts.

Where is everyone? There're always people running

round the trim trail or little kids splashing about. Why is there no one to be seen at all, the one time when it really matters?

'Help!' I shout again. 'Lamont! Beaky! Help me!'

But they don't answer. If Lamont *was* here, he'd know what to do. He actually knows how to do resuscitation from when the lady from the St John's Ambulance came in to teach us life-saving. Beaky and me got the giggles when we had to give the plastic dummy the kiss of life and Mr Pasco sent us out. Why didn't I stop messing around and listen?

I tap the boy's cheek.

'Wake up!' I say desperately. 'Please!'

That bird squawks again.

'Wake up!' I grab his shoulder and I shake him. Hard. 'WAKE UP!' I shout.

The boy's eyes flicker open and look straight into mine. His eyes are so dark I see myself reflected there.

Then he rolls over and coughs so hard that water comes spurting up. He gasps in air but that only makes him cough even more. He drags himself on to all fours and coughs and retches and spits until it all comes out. His head hangs limply between his arms, his long, dark hair brushes the ground and the blood from the cut on his head drips steadily on to the sand. I hear him breathe, shallow rattling breaths. I see his ribs moving beneath his sandy skin, as if breathing is really hard work.

For the first time I look at the boy properly. He's wearing animal skins on his bottom half and his top half is bare. He's thin and wiry, his legs and arms criss-crossed with scratches, but he's strong-looking too. A few string bracelets are tied around his wrists. Then I see his hands, pressed hard into the sand. They're big, broad, long-fingered, powerful hands. As if he can feel me staring, the boy whips his head to the side and glares at me through his long wet hair.

'Who are you?' I say.

# SPEA

'Are you OK? Where do you live? Are you lost?'

The boy doesn't answer, he just stares at me hard, angry, almost accusing. His eyes are like black holes.

He takes a big wheezy breath, then he starts to speak, but his voice is rough and rasping. Low like a growl and I don't understand.

Who you? Who you? You boy? You girl? I not know you! Who you?

I shake my head at him. 'I have no idea what you're saying.' His voice gets louder, faster, like he's cross.

WHO you? You push me in river? You make me fall? You want kill me dead?

'Calm down. Please. It's OK.'

But he doesn't calm down. He starts really yelling,

thumping his chest as he speaks.

YOU WANT KILL ME DEAD!

I kill YOU dead! Ha!

I not fraid you! HA!

He awkwardly staggers to his feet, and peers about like he's searching for something. Then he fixes me with his dark angry glare. I back away.

Where my spea? You TAKE my spea? Where my SPEA?

*Spea!* I hear, half understanding maybe. 'Did you just say *spear*?'

But before I have time to think the boy suddenly leaps forward, springing at me like an attack. I stumble back but not fast enough; he lifts a quick hand and grabs hold of the pocket of my soggy blue T-shirt.

'Hey!' I yell, pulling away, trying to tug myself free. 'Get off me!'

He doesn't though; he holds on tighter; his nails are filthy black.

You push me in river! You take my spea! I kill you dead!

'What? What are you saying? Let go!' I grab my T-shirt and pull back. He yanks hard and my pocket rips off in his big hand. I stagger backwards again.

'What d'you do that for?' I say, shocked and furious.

The boy looks at the torn-off pocket in his hand, then back to me. Suddenly he roars, his eyes narrow with vicious fury. He leaps at me again.

Screaming, I turn and run back along the beach towards the reeds. But when I don't hear him at my heels, I glance back.

The boy is lying in a crumpled heap on the sand like a dropped puppet. Has he collapsed? Or is he just pretending? Trying to trap me into going back to check on him ... and then ... BAM ... he'll pounce on me again? Playing dead.

My heart's thudding like an engine. I look around again for Beaky and Lamont. Where are they when I need them? I squeeze myself into the reeds and crouch down so that I'm hidden. I watch the boy. Why did he attack me? What's the matter with him?

I'm hiding right next to the river pool where I found him; I look at the rock where the boy bashed his head – its jagged tip is still red with his blood; it looks like a miniature model of an erupting volcano. How did he end up in the river anyway? And did he just ... slip over or ... ? My imagination whirs with possibilities, all of them awful. And then I notice something: there, jammed between the jagged rock and its neighbour, is a long pale stick, unusual-looking, sharp at one end. A breeze rustles the reeds.

'A spear?' I whisper.

Cautiously, keeping my eye on the boy, I wade into the shallow water, free the spear and pick it up. It's beautiful, as tall as me and made from wood whittled white, with all the bark stripped off. At its tip the pointed spearhead is held fast to the shaft with twists of twine. I look closer and I see that it's a flint, carved to a point, just like the microlith I have in my collection at home. Tentatively, I reach up and press my finger to the tip of the spearhead; it's as sharp as a claw. This isn't a toy. This is a real spear.

I hold the spear in the middle, where I imagine the boy holds it because the shaft here is more smoothed and worn. My hand fits his handhold perfectly. I move the spear back and forth above my shoulder, like it's a javelin.

'Speeeaaa!' I say quietly, trying out the shape of the boy's odd voice.

I look back towards the boy's crumpled body. Why is he running around in Mandel Forest dressed in animal skins and carrying a spear? He still hasn't moved.

Little bubbles of worry rise up from my belly. I'm worried the boy might attack me, but I'm even more worried he might actually be dying. That can happen with drowning – Mum told me – you can nearly drown and then you seem perfectly OK for ages but a bit of water got trapped in your lungs without you even knowing and it drowns you later when you're back on dry land. Horrible!

Cautiously, I creep back across the river beach towards him, feet squelching in my wet trainers. I feel braver now, with this spear in my hand.

I stand by the boy. A lizard darts across the sand, past the boy's bare foot. His feet are like his hands, broad and strong. His right ankle is all puffed up and swollen. His long hair has fallen half across his face, revealing a big oozing cut on his forehead. He has a wide nose and high cheekbones and his eyes are closed. He has long, dark eyelashes. With my toe I nudge his foot, ever so gently, but he just lies there motionless. I bite my lip.

Slowly I crouch down next to him, heart thudding with dread.

# BAD SPIRIT?

A shrill cry pierces the still air. I jump out of my skin. The cry comes again; a bird, but not one I recognise; it sounds just like a tiny baby. Just like Dara. The bird cries again.

The boy does a huge jolt like he's been electrified. It gives me such a shock, I fall back on to the sand. He starts thrashing his head from side to side. He's alive!

Relief floods through me. Relief mingled with fear. I grip the spear more tightly and shuffle out of his reach, in case he wakes up properly.

'Mmmmmmffffaaa,' mumbles the boy, his eyes still closed. 'Mmmmmfffggaa.'

Then he gets louder, calling out deliriously in his sleep in his language that I don't understand.

MOTHGIRL!

Mothgirl! Make safe! MAKE SAFE!
MOTHGIRL!

'Mothga?' I murmur, shaking my head. What does
*Mothga* mean?

His eyes shoot open. He sees me. My heart starts to
thud. I shuffle away from him fast, holding white-
knuckle-tight to the spear.

'Hey!' I say, trying to keep my voice level. 'Hey! Just
be calm. It's OK.'

But the boy doesn't look OK. He scuffles to his feet
and skitters away from me towards the ridge which
separates the beach from the forest. He's making a circle
shape, like a telescope, with one fist and shouting words I
don't understand in his strange gruff voice:

WHO YOU? I not know you.
You bad? You bad bad spirit?
BAD SPIRIT!
You take my spea!
You put your bad spirit curses on me!
GO YOU! Go you, Bad Spirit! Leave me!
Go back to your bad bad land!

He yells and yells at me, but his voice is more like
growls. Furious. Ferocious. Wild.

Suddenly he stops shouting and stands stock-still, like

69

we all used to do when we played musical statues at birthday parties. What's he doing?

A shrill cry pierces the air – it's that bird that sounds like a baby. The cry fades. The boy turns back to me and, fire-eyed, he roars:

WHERE MOTHGIRL?
I hear Mothgirl cry!
Where you take my Mothgirl?
Tell me now, Bad Spirit!
Tell me now or I kill you dead!
Where MY Mothgirl?

'Moth-ga?' I say. It's that word again. 'I don't understand you.'

He picks up a stone. 'MOTHGAAA!' he yells as he hurls it at me. It misses, but only just.

'Oi!' I say, but my voice comes out in a little squeak. I grip the spear more tightly. 'What're you playing at? I'm trying to help you!'

Where you take my Mothgirl, Bad Spirit? he shouts, picking up another stone, a bigger one.

'Stop it!' I squeak. 'I don't know what you're saying!' I've backed away from him so much, I'm ankle-deep in water.

A wood pigeon rises noisily out of the trees behind the

boy, the sudden rustle and fluster makes me jump out of my skin. I see the boy jump too; that surprises me.

Something suddenly occurs to me: I take a step forward, towards the boy. He draws back, wide-eyed.

Unbelievable! In spite of all his yelling and his gruff voice and that big rock he's brandishing, this fierce boy is actually frightened ... He's frightened of *me*.

# CONK CUSHION

The pigeon flies away over the river. We face each other, the boy and I, and our eyes lock. 'WHHHHOOOOO-WHHHhhooooooo,' calls the pigeon as it passes over our heads.

The tiniest haziest inkling of a memory flashes in my mind. The boy's voice. His strange growly voice. I recognise it. I've heard that voice before …

The boy's staring at me differently now too. He slowly lowers the hand with the rock in it and points at me, blinking; he's mumbling quietly to himself, like he's in a trance, in a dream world.

You not bad spirit! I know you. I see you before.

I member: I sit in hazel tree. I hunt.

I wait. I wait. I wait.

I sleep?

Sleep story come. I see you in my sleep story.

You stand under hazel tree.

I watch you.

Choll-ie-murr-um.

Yes. I see you before, Cholliemurrum!

Cholliemurrum.

Speaking softly, unsure, I echo the boy's word back at him. 'Chollie-murrum?' It's the word I heard whispered in Mandel Forest last night. I *do* recognise that voice; it's the voice I thought I heard. The voice which almost said my name. 'Charlie Merriam?' I say.

Cholliemurrum, agrees the boy, pointing across at me. He looks almost as gobsmacked as I am.

'Cholliemurrum,' I say, like it actually is my name. And I get such a funny feeling, deep in my head near my back teeth, like ... like ... the little click a key makes as it turns perfectly in its lock. I give my head a joggle. It feels like my ears have popped and everything sounds clearer, better.

I point at myself. 'Cholliemurrum,' I say again. 'And who are *you*?' I ask, pointing to him now.

He stares down at himself, examines his own big hands, then touches his own face.

His eyes meet mine as he slowly, sadly shakes his head. 'I not know me,' he says in a husky whisper. 'I not member me.'

And I hear him properly. I actually understand him suddenly. Clear as air.

'Oh … You don't remember … do you?' I say softly, and then I get why he's so odd and confused and frightened. He's lost his memory. 'Don't worry, you banged your head, that's all.' I touch my own head in the place where his cut is.

As if he's only just noticed it he reaches up and feels the dark oozy gash across his forehead. 'Yoooo make this?' he says in horror, looking down at his bloody fingertips, staggering backwards.

'No! No! Of course I didn't. I just found you. I found you in the water and I …'

I hesitate, what just happened catching up with me suddenly. '… I … I saved you … I think …' I don't quite believe it myself; I've never saved anyone before. I smile at the boy, dazed, proud almost.

He doesn't smile back, instead he ignores me; he's fiddling with one of the twisted string bracelets on his wrist. 'Mothga …' he murmurs, stroking the bracelet

74

tenderly. 'I member Mothga …' His eyes flick back to me, fast and accusing. 'Where Mothga? You take Mothga, Cholliemurrum?'

I shake my head. 'No. I don't know what you're on about. What's Mothga? '

The boy gazes sadly at the string bracelet. 'Mothga my sister. Mothga my baby sister.'

'Baby sister,' I echo softly. My heart pangs and a strange ache pulls at the pit of my stomach.

I see a sudden cloud of remembering cross the boy's eyes. 'Mothga!' he shouts, looking all about in a panic. 'Where Mothga? Mothga all alone! I need make safe! Fast! Fast!'

Before I can say or do anything, he leaps to his feet and instantly his face turns ghost pale; his eyes roll back and he collapses in a heap again like he's melted.

I run over to him. He's OK, he's breathing thickly; he just fainted I think. I stare at his blood-streaked, sandy face. What's wrong with him?

A memory pings into my head.

*Concussion?* I think to myself, from when he bashed his head on the rock. Beaky had concussion once, when she fell off the climbing frame in primary school. She called it *conk-cushion* afterwards, when she was better. But it wasn't even slightly funny at the time. She was properly knocked out and she just lay there in the playzone, really still and pale so we knew she wasn't pretending. Then when she woke up she didn't know Lamont or me at all; she just stared at us like we were strangers. I remember how she screamed and shouted *Go away!* at us. That was the scariest part. She didn't even know who we were or who she was or anything. Mrs Rodriguez had to call an ambulance.

An ambulance! That's what I need. If only Mum and Dad *had* got me a phone then it'd be easy. I scan up and down the river for Beaky, Lamont … anyone … but there's still nobody.

'OK,' I say to the boy, whether he can hear me or not. 'I'm going to get help.' I straighten Dad's backpack on my shoulders, then I scramble on to the ridge and run towards the path back up through the forest to the hospital.

But I stop dead in my tracks; the path is gone.

# THE PINNACLE

I stare at the place where the path should be. This can't be right. I scan left and right along the forest edge, but there are only trees.

'What?' I say. 'Where … ?'

With a shaky hand I use the spear to lift the hanging fronds of fern and ivy where the path used to be. I take a sharp breath. There's no sign that anyone has ever passed this way before. But … I ran down here myself only twenty minutes ago … didn't I?

I peer into the forest shadows, breathing fast; it all looks different somehow: darker, greener, thick with briars and tangleweed. Even the air is strange; it has a heavy, flowery stink, too sickly sweet, like mouldy rottenness. I try to breathe through my mouth as I stare into the twisting undergrowth, searching desperately. It's as if the path has been swallowed up by the forest.

'Haaaa! Haaaaa! Haaaaaaa!' taunts a bird from high in the canopy.

The forest squawks and buzzes and hums with noises like I've never heard before, even in midsummer. An animal shriek rises from somewhere ahead of me, like something in pain. I freeze. What even was that? Mandel Forest is like my home but suddenly nothing is familiar and I'm afraid.

I look back over my shoulder at the boy, still lying where he fell. I glance down at the pale spear in my hand. I listen to the harsh *chakka-chakka* chatter of a bird I don't recognise. A strange thought strikes me then: maybe that boy's not the one who's lost; maybe I am. Panic presses down on me like a cold weight as I walk to the river's edge, my head spinning.

I know this place, but I don't know it. How can that be? The river looks more or less the same, but ... there's no bridge. I can't believe I didn't notice that before! How can a whole bridge just disappear? I gaze upstream, and my heart leaps: there *is* something I recognise.

I race along the beach to the stepping stones, where the river runs shallowest, and I rock hop until I'm at the highest boulder, the one that's right in the middle of the river. We call it the Pinnacle, Beaky, Lamont and me. The Pinnacle's almost as tall as the Spirit Stone but less smooth and more craggy; easier to climb, and as I scramble up, it feels just as it should – the footholds and handholds are all in their same normal places. I stand on the flat bit at the top of the Pinnacle staring around me.

What is going on?

All I see is endless green; too much green. Not even a bench or a signpost, or a glimpse of rooftops above the treeline. Nothing is right.

But then my heart soars: high up on the hill behind the beach I see the Spirit Stone, right where it always is, like an old friend. I turn and face the other way, across the river from where the boy lies ... hoping ... hoping as I peer through the rippling thickness of trees ... and ... yes! There it is! Half hidden in the undergrowth, I can just make out the open black mouth of Deadman's Cave.

This *is* still my forest after all! Well, it is ... and it isn't. A breeze trembles through the leaves, the softest whisper. The hairs on my neck prickle.

Suddenly an idea strikes me ... What if ... what if ... I've entered another version of my world? Gone through a portal or something into another dimension – like in *Doctor Who*! Then I stop myself.

'Don't be ridiculous, Charlie,' I mutter, and I almost smile, because without even meaning to, I'm doing an impression of grumpy Mr Pasco, our science teacher. Mr Pasco's about ninety-five and he doesn't like me one bit. 'Charlie is somewhat prone to flights of fancy,' he said to Dad on parents' evening, only last week. I took it as a compliment.

Parents' evening! Dad! Mum! I twist and turn my head, frantically searching for something familiar as panic rises all fluttery in my chest: Mum and Dad are going to absolutely kill me. I squint my eyes towards where the hospital should be … but it's not there, of course it's not there – no hospital, no town, just endless endless forever forest. And on the horizon purply-grey clouds are bubbling: ominous, like a storm is on its way.

I stand on the Pinnacle and try to think. What would Lamont do? He's 'got common sense' as Mum always says.

I make a list in my head, adding up the facts like Lamont would:

1. Right now, for whatever crazy reason, I'm lost: everything is different … and I don't know how to make it normal again.

2. The only other person I've seen since everything changed is that boy.
3. But the boy is injured. He needs help …
4. But I need help! *I* need to get back home again.

The facts don't even sound like facts! And they certainly don't add up. They just spiral about the place like a big old mess. What am I going to do?

# HELP YOU

I slip down off the Pinnacle and cross back over to the
boy on the beach.

I crouch next to him, listening. His breath bubbles like
his lungs are still half-full of water. The cut on his forehead is dark and oozy and I flick away a fly. A thin cloud
passes across the sun and suddenly the boy's black-hole
eyes shoot open. I draw back.

'Cold,' he whispers. His voice is thin, his lips purple.
It's like all the fight has drained out of him and he doesn't
look vicious any more; he just looks really sick.

I realise I have no choice. 'Don't worry. I'm going to
help you.'

'Help you?' he echoes, and for a second his eyes meet
mine. 'Help you,' he says again weakly.

He reaches fast, grabs my hand, stares at me hard; his eyes are glazed and fearful. 'Mothga,' he says, and even though his voice trembles I hear him clearly. 'Mothga. Make. Safe.' His eyelids flicker and his eyes roll so that I can only see the whites, then they close again.

'Mothga. Make safe?' I repeat quietly to myself. Mothga? A chilly breeze blows ripples in the river. I shiver. 'I don't know how to help you,' I whisper to the boy.

I lay the pale spear on the sand by my side, then I shake off Dad's backpack and rummage for something … something … helpful. For once I'm glad Dad's too disorganised to ever clear out his bag, because, down beneath all the *un*helpful somethings – the battered book, the empty water bottle, the pencils and receipts and chocolate wrappers and other rubbish – right down at the very bottom, all squished and crumpled, is one of his old checked shirts. That'll keep the boy warm. I pull it out, give it a shake and, just for a second, I cuddle it close; it's soft and warm and it smells like Dad.

The boy mutters but doesn't wake as I tuck Dad's shirt over him like a blanket. He shifts a little in his sleep and does a deep rattly sigh, like Dad's shirt makes *him* feel safer too.

I shoo away the flies buzzing around the boy's face and take a closer look at the sticky cut on his forehead. It's deep and speckled with sand and mud. If it's not infected yet it soon will be. I remember when our old cat King Tut walked on something sharp once and his paw got infected. He got really sick; it was horrible. Yes, I need to clean up that cut. I look around for something to do it with.

In his other hand the boy is holding something blue; it's the pocket he ripped off my T-shirt. Gently, never taking my eyes off his face, I peel open his fingers. I soak the pocket in the river and squeeze it out.

'This might sting a bit,' I say softly. I wince as the water dribbles into the wound. I'm as gentle as I can be but the boy moans and twists his head from side to side. Luckily I don't think he's got enough strength to do anything more. Feeling braver, I slosh more water on to his head until the cut is nice and clean.

'All done!'

Already his head looks so much better. And I'm sure the colour is starting to come back to his cheeks now he's warming up. I rinse out the bloody pocket and tear another strip of fabric from round the bottom of my T-shirt. I hold the pocket on the cut and wrap the blue strip around his head as tightly as I can.

'There!' I lean back on my heels and admire my handi-
work. Not a bad bandage actually. Even if I have made
him look a bit like a pirate. My laugh surprises me.

The boy opens his eyes; well, he opens one of them.
He can't fully open his left eye because of the bandage
and that makes him look even more wonky and pirate-
ish. I giggle again.

'Sorry,' I say, gently adjusting the bandage. Slowly his
eyes swim into focus.

I see the moment when he sees me properly; he does
a little jolt and his black eyes fill with that dangerous,
frightened gleam again. My heart starts to thud. I shuffle
away from him fast, grabbing the spear.

'Hello,' I say, trying to keep my voice level. 'Hello! I'm
Charlie, I'm trying to help you, remember?'

He narrows his eyes suspiciously.

I try again. 'It's me … Cholliemurrum.'

His gaze clears. He touches his head, where my wonky
blue bandage is. 'You make this, Cholliemurrum?' I can't
tell if he's happy or cross about my homemade bandage.

'Um … Yes …' I say hesitantly, hoping it's the right
answer and it won't make him go all bananas again.

'Good,' he says, like he's marking me for my skills or
something.

'Thanks,' I say, almost giggling, but he's so serious I don't dare.

Lightning. A sudden flash; I only see it out of the corner of my eye, almost like it was never there at all. Nervously, I look up at the cloud-heavy sky and I listen. The wind is rising. I hear the low growl of thunder.

The boy's eyes widen as he too stares skywards. 'Ssstorrmm voys,' he whispers.

'Storm voice,' I whisper back, understanding.

Another flash and the first fat drops of rain start to fall.

# TRUST ME

A gust of wind whirls up, lifting my hair, blowing the river back upon itself, swaying the treetops. Three crows flap untidily past, flying away from the storm. Lightning.

One.

Two.

Three.

Four.

Fi—

Thunder. The storm is less than five kilometres away.

'Sstorm close,' says the boy, crouching now, watching the sky.

The rain is getting heavier. We can't be out here in the open when the storm hits us properly – we'll get struck by lightning; we need to shelter. I look across the river at the black open mouth of Deadman's Cave.

I hesitate. Should we? My mum and Lamont's mum have banned us from going into Deadman's Cave. Beaky said it was because there was a hermit living in there who didn't want to be disturbed by a bunch of kids. Lamont said it was more likely because Shim Carter and his mates all hung out in the cave drinking cider and breaking bottles and listening to music really loud.

The sky darkens ominously. Deadman's Cave will be perfect.

'Look, listen, I know a place we can be safe. A cave.'

'Kaaayfff?' says the boy, shaking his head. 'What kaaayff?'

I point across the river. 'That cave, over there.'

The boy looks from me to where I'm pointing and back to me again.

'No, Cholliemurrum,' he says, getting himself to his feet, more carefully this time. Dad's shirt falls on to the sand. 'I find Mothga.' He folds his arms stubbornly across his chest. 'No kaaayff!'

'Yes cave! This is a bad place to be in a storm. You can find Mothga later. Come with me. Trust me.'

He screws up his eyes, concentrating; squinting at me,

as if he's trying to see through a dirty window. 'Rust-me?' He teeters, unsteady still on his feet.

'Yes. Trust me.' I hold out my hand towards him, beckoning for him to take it.

The sky is so black now it feels like night is falling, and the rain's properly splattering too. 'Come on! Hurry up!'

The boy takes another staggery step away from me, blinking suspiciously. Thunder booms. The storm's coming in really fast, it'll reach us soon.

Then I have an idea. I know what'll help him trust me. I roll the spear towards him along the ground. The boy snatches up his spear, and glares at me. Trickles of blood-tinged rain are running down the sides of his face and his hair is stuck to his cheek. The boy's eyes narrow. Lightning lights us up, jittery and awful, and the spear in the boy's hand flashes bone white. Thunder crashes and bangs almost overhead. Suddenly, I realise that I might have just made a huge mistake. What was I thinking? This boy's not my friend; I've no idea who he is or what's happened to him ... or what he might do next.

'I trust you,' I say, but my voice has gone all squeaky and unconvincing.

Lightning flashes in a huge zigzag across the black sky. Thunder crashes like the world is breaking. The boy stares at me, his eyelids flickering. He can't pass out again; not here, not now.

'Please!' I say, and our eyes lock.

He rams his spear into the sand and leans on it like a walking stick. 'Peas,' he says solemnly, and he starts to stumble towards me. 'I come kayyfff!'

I laugh. A mad, scared, electric laugh. 'Hurry up then,' I say in relief, 'before we both get frazzled.'

I go to the boy and hold out my hand to help him; he doesn't take it, but he does hobble closer to my side, still leaning on his spear, so that when, in a new touch of dizziness, he starts to sway I can put my arm out to steady him.

'Just hold on to me!' I have to shout over another crash of thunder.

He puts his heavy hand on my shoulder. He grips it so tight I almost wince; his fingers feel like claws. And that's how, together, we cross the river through the pelting rain: me, Charlie Merriam, and him, this wild, unpredictable boy.

We step off the last stepping stone and our feet squelch down into the ooze of mud. The boy drops his hold of me and leans back on to a tree trunk. I lean next to him, and we stand still a moment, both of us breathing hard. The air tastes sharp and electric, full of storm shivers. I sense the boy looking at me. I peek at him out of the corner of my eye too and a little tingle zigzags through my bones. Thunder booms.

The storm is deadly close now; looking up I see the treetops bend and wave in the wind.

'Let's go. Quick!' I pat my shoulder for him to hold on to, but he tosses his head in refusal, with that proud, stubborn look on his face again.

'Fine then, be like that,' I mutter as I squelch hurriedly through the riverside mud just ahead of him, leading us towards the cave.

We've gone about a dozen footsteps when the next lightning flash crackles so close it makes my hair prickle. Instinctively, I start to run. I look back over my shoulder at the boy and he's trying to run too, lolloping awkwardly on his bad leg. Then I gasp in horror. Behind the boy, the lightning finds its target; it reaches out of the black sky like a jabbing finger and strikes that tree we were only just leaning on.

I freeze, transfixed for a second by the beautiful horror of it as the tree is lit up from the inside out, branches turned white like bones in an X-ray. With a monstrous tearing sound the lightning-struck tree starts to lean towards us.

'It's falling!' I scream, but the creak and wrench and crash drown out my voice.

# STORM VOICE

The boy yells, he grabs my arm. And we're running then, holding tight to each other, desperately slipping and sliding across the mud. Lightning jitters make everything juddery like a strobe light flickering and I can't see properly. I feel the whoosh of wind at our heels and the dark gape of the cave mouth is suddenly just in front of us. I drag the boy in behind me and we dive together on to the floor of Deadman's Cave. The tree hits the ground outside with an almighty splintering thud; I feel its reverberations in the whole of my body as I lie, belly-down, on the cool rock. The air I breathe smells singed, like woodsmoke and fireworks.

I sit up slowly, dazed, spitting bits of muck from my mouth. My ears ring. I feel the boy's eyes watching me in the half-dark. I turn to face him.

'Cholliemurrum,' he says quietly, sitting up too. His face looks almost old suddenly in his seriousness. He takes his spear and touches its glinting flint tip to his chest, right where his heart would be. 'I give thanks,' he whispers. He touches his spear tip to my chest too. I feel the cool of it through my damp T-shirt. But I don't pull away, I don't need to, I trust him. I understand. 'I give thanks,' he says again.

'No worries. Anytime,' I answer. A little tear trickles out of the corner of my eye. I brush it away quickly before he sees, my fingers trembling like crazy.

Turning away, I squint out of the cave through the net of fallen-tree branches and the sheets of rain. Lightning crackles, making the forest flicker like an old old film; I wince at the brightness. Thunder crashes so loud it echoes in my heart.

Usually I love storms. But I don't love this one. I love storms when I'm safe at home, cuddled up with Mum and Dad. Going 'Oooooh' and 'Aaaaah!' like it's some sort of massive firework display. A big wave of sadness rises in my chest. 'I want to go home,' I whisper. I want to be safe; I want to be looked after.

Thunder booms, long and hollow. 'Storm voice,' I murmur as I look down and a tear drips on to my goosebumpy arm. I wipe it away. I wonder what time it really is? I wonder how long I've been gone? I wonder if up at the hospital window they're all watching the storm … I wonder, are they missing me too? I rub at my pathetic tears with the end of my T-shirt. How am I going to get home?

Lightning jabs through the sky. I squeeze my eyes tight to try to shut out the storm and the cave. I imagine hearing a team of park rangers in high-vis jackets shouting my name; I imagine hearing them huffing and puffing through the undergrowth towards Deadman's Cave. I imagine the glare of their torch beams finding me here in the gloom. 'So here's where you've been hiding!' they say, and they give me hot chocolate out of a flask and one of those shiny foil blankets. Then they radio Mum and Dad to tell them that it's all fine; they've found me; I'm OK.

But I'm not OK, am I? A huge crash of thunder makes me open my eyes. It's all just the same. The storm still swirls through the strange, wild forest.

I gasp, my breath catching in my throat.

Over on the beach side of the river. There's someone there! A shadow, running fast through the blur of rain.

# DEADMAN'S CAVE

'Hey!' I call, scrambling up to my feet. 'Hey! You!'

The shadow pauses for a second. I wave, squinting through the blanket of thick rain. 'Hey! Hey! Come here, help us!' But I don't think he can hear me; he grabs something from the beach, then the shadow vanishes into the trees.

I spring forward, forcing back the topmost branches of the fallen tree. I shove my way out into the rain. 'Come back!' I shout. But my voice is squashed tiny by the pounding rain and the crashing thunder.

I blink, rub my eyes. Nothing there. He's gone. Then I start to doubt myself. Was the shadow just a stupid imagining? A trick of the light?

'Did *you* see that?' I say quietly to the boy.

But he doesn't answer. He has shuffled himself back into a little hollow by the cave mouth. His eyes are closed and his breath is raspy. As I step back into Deadman's Cave the cave wall behind the boy flashes bright with lightning. 'Oh!' I breathe, awestruck, clapping my hand over my mouth at what I see.

It's not possible. I know this cave. This isn't possible.

The walls of Deadman's Cave are absolutely covered with pictures; paintings that seem to move like a flick book in the jittering light.

The lightning fades again. But I have to see more! I tear off Dad's backpack and rummage about; I find his torch and click the switch.

'Oh, Dad!' I hiss through my teeth. The battery's dead, of course. Mum's always telling Dad off for not changing the batteries on things. 'For goodness sake, Dad, you total banana!' I bang the torch on my hand. It flickers to life, a thin, pale beam, but it's enough. I hold the torch high and peer all around me at the painted walls of Deadman's Cave.

They're not just pictures, they're pictures that tell stories: there's a hunter who bounds long-legged in a leap. The hunter's chasing a red deer, a hart with massive antlers, and the deer's fast too, I can feel the strength of its muscles in the curve of the line. And there's another deer ahead, a young one, smaller antlers, less strong, less sure; he's looking back over his shoulder. But the young deer doesn't see the hunter or the spear, the spear that's arcing from the hunter's empty hand, straight towards the deer's panicky heart. 'Spea!' I murmur. The torch fades and goes out.

'Come on!' I bang the torch on the cave wall. I want to see more. Trembly thin light wavers through the gloom.

'Wow!' I whisper, walking a few steps deeper into the cave, forgetting myself at the sheer wonder of it. These walls are alive with eagles that swoop and fish that leap. I see lynx and bear and elk and wolf and other animals whose names I don't even know. Living pictures of creatures long gone from *my* Mandel Forest. And there are more people, people just like the boy with wild hair and animal skins, clutching spears in quick, strong hands. 'Chauvet!' I whisper. 'Lascaux.' Because I'm remembering the pictures in *The Wild*; photos of famous caves in France with paintings just like these ones, thousands and thousands of years old. 'Stone Age paintings,' I murmur as my torch fizzles out properly. All is blackness. Outside thunder booms.

I can feel the truth sitting beside me in the dark, watching me, waiting, daring me to meet its stare.

'I'm in the Stone Age, aren't I?' I whisper; I'm breathing quickly. The air is cold; it tastes of damp and moss and mushrooms; the cave drips steadily like the ticking of a clock. 'I'm in the Stone Age.' A tingle of fear and excitement surges through me.

'And you,' I breathe, squinting through the dim at the vague outline of the boy's sleeping shape. 'You're from here. You're ... you're a real Stone Age boy.' I shudder and I giggle and I hiccup all at the same time; my insides fizz and my brain spins.

Then I hear something. A new something. I slowly turn my head and I listen. There's a noise coming from way way back behind me, right in the depths of Deadman's Cave.

# GROWL

'Is there anybody here?' My voice sounds shrill in the dark.

The only answer is the rush of my own heartbeat.

Fear steals through me, cold and shivery.

There it is again. A tiny whimpering noise; almost like a ... *a kitten*. That's what I tell myself anyway, forcing myself to think of the least scary thing I can imagine. For a second I hesitate, blinking in the darkness, then I hurry back towards the mouth of the cave. But my foot catches on a sticky-uppy rock and I fall hard, flinging my hands out to save myself.

My palms sting as they slap the stony floor and my breath's all knocked out of me. I sit up, struggling to breathe. I touch my knee: sticky, it's bleeding. The cave water trickles; it sounds almost like a little giggle, laughing at me in the blackness. I put my hand on my chest and take deep breaths, trying to calm myself.

From the depths of the cave I hear the whimpering sound again and suddenly I realise what it actually does sound like – it sounds just like …

'… a baby?' I whisper.

The boy's baby sister. Mothga?

I stagger to my feet, wincing at the pain in my knee.

Then I hear something which turns my blood to ice. A growl, low and steady, and it's close. I look up; a huge dog stands silhouetted in the cave entrance.

I hold my breath … maybe it's just a nice friendly dog, like Nero.

The dog's growl deepens. I swallow, thinking of all the wild animals I saw in the cave paintings: there were no nice friendly dogs in the Stone Age, were there? My breathing quickens. It's not a dog; it's a wolf.

The wolf pads into the cave. He lowers his huge body to the ground and slinks towards me, his growl deep and steady. I'm paralysed with fear but, even if I could move, the wolf's blocking my escape. My breath comes back in quick bursts. I can't get out! I can't get out! I smell a metallic smell, like iron, like blood. The growl rises to a snarl and I glimpse the white of the wolf's teeth in a lightning flash. I need to do something, run deeper into the cave maybe; see if there's another way out.

The wolf stops snarling, throws back his head and howls. It's so loud I can feel it reverberating in my bones; I cover my ears, burying my face in my arms.

'Aloooo-ooooo-oooooone?' he howls. But he isn't. Because from all across the forest howls answer howls until the air almost ripples with it.

The wolf isn't alone. I am.

I crouch on the floor, trying not cry, trying not to breathe, trying not to smell like food.

The wolf turns to stare out of the cave, sniffs the stormy air. His ears twitch. Maybe he hasn't seen me after all. Maybe he'll just go off to join the pack.

It's OK. It's OK, I tell myself. I've read stuff about wolves. Wolves only attack people really really rarely. I've definitely read that in *The Wild*; you've got less chance of being attacked by a wolf than of being hit by lightning. I gulp, looking at the silhouetted branches of the storm-struck tree.

Then I hear it again; that high, mewling sound, from somewhere deep in the cave dark. Instantly, the wolf turns back to me. He drops to the ground and slowly,

slowly comes closer, ears flattened, tail low, silent. He moves out of the dim light at the cave's edge and into my darkness. He's even more terrifying when you can't see him. I hear the *click click click* of his claws on the floor.

I try to swallow but my mouth's too dry. I daren't breathe but I know the worst thing I could do is panic. I try to think about what else I know about wolves. If a wolf does threaten you, you're supposed to either act bigger than them, scare them off, or you're supposed to act smaller than them, so they don't feel threatened. The wolf's growl deepens, so low I feel it in my belly. Which one was it? Act big or act small? I can't remember! What am I supposed to do?

I decide to act big.

I jump to my feet and shout as loud as I can.

## WOLF

'Get out, wolf! Get out! Go home!'

My voice bounces off the walls of the cave. '... *home ...*
*home ... home ...*'

The wolf's growl turns into a snarl.

'RRRAAAAAAAA!' I yell back.

Paws on stone.

*Click*

*Click*

*Click*

'Go away!' I yell again, my voice cracking. 'Get away
from me!'

I scramble back, away from the thin band of daylight,
deeper into the dark. I can't see the wolf but I can hear him,
his growl low and steady, more like a vibration than a sound.

My back bumps into the wall and I can feel the cold dampness creeping through my T-shirt. I whimper, my breath ragged and catching in my throat.

'Go home!' I scream desperately at the wolf, and he's so close I can smell his warm stink in the air between us.

*Home!* All I want is to go home ...

A scurry of pebbles. The tiniest cold breeze.

The weight of the wolf, all fur and muscle, knocks me sideways. Winded, flat on my back, I smell the stench of the wolf's hot, meaty breath. His dreadful growl goes right through me, into my bones. I feel my lungs fill with air and I scream. I thrash and writhe and try to shove him away. My fingers sink deep in his thick fur; I grab a handful in each fist and try to wrestle him off me. The wolf shakes his head and I lose my grip. I tighten my hands and punch with all my strength. The wolf snarls and pins me down; his claws dig into my shoulders like knives. I start to kick and kick my legs, but the wolf doesn't shift at all.

I scream. I sound like a small animal. I sound like prey.

I hear a thunk and a thrum. The wolf lets out a yelp and falls hot and heavy on top of me, thrashing his head from side and side and snapping his jaws. I try to wriggle out from beneath him but his writhing body keeps me pinned to the ground. I get my right arm free and shield my face from his gnashing jaws. I feel him weakening and with my right arm and both my legs I shove, using all my strength, and the wolf rolls off me on to the floor. There's a creak and a splintery snap, like a branch is breaking and, from inside the wolf's body, a terrible tearing sound. The wolf sighs and is still.

I lie there, next to the dead wolf, panting. I open and close my hands, flex my trembling fingers. Everything hurts but I'm alive. It doesn't seem possible. I nearly died. That was almost the end. But somehow ... I'm still here ... alive ... OK.

I hear raspy breathing and struggle to sit up in the darkness.

'Who's there?' I whisper.

# I GIVE THANKS

A rattly cough.

'Cholliemurrum?' mutters the boy's gruff voice.

Suddenly my eyes fill up with tears. I sniff and bite my lip but the tears pour out anyway and I sob so hard I'm shaking all over.

'You cry, Cholliemurrum?' asks the boy's voice in the dark.

'Yes,' I say, my own voice all strange and choked.

'Not cry, Cholliemurrum.' The boy speaks softly.

I hear his limping footsteps coming towards me, see his tear-blurred outline silhouetted in the yellowish storm light. He sits down beside me in the dark; I can feel the warmth of him and smell his human smell. I turn to face him. I open my mouth to speak but no words come out.

'Not cry, Cholliemurrum,' says the boy again, and he touches my wet cheek. His skin is rough but he's gentle.

I shudder and I cry and I feel like I'll never be able to stop.

'Wolf breath gone, Cholliemurrum,' says the boy.

I feel his hand grasp mine and pull it gently towards the wolf's lifeless body. I try to draw back but the boy holds on tightly, guiding my hand across the wolf's furry belly. His hand shows my hand a place where the wolf's fur is warm and sticky with blood; I curl back my fingers but his hand holds me there.

'Wolf in spirit sleep,' whispers the boy. 'I kill wolf dead.'

'I know,' I say, sniffing. 'Thank you.'

I stretch out my fingers and wrap them tightly around the smooth wooden spear, imagining that it was me who had thrown it, swift and true through the dark. The boy puts his big hand around mine. Together we wrench the spear free.

The boy lays his palm on the wolf's wound.

'I give thanks,' he says. For a moment I think he's thanking me, but then I realise he's talking to the wolf.

'Why?' I say, wiping my eyes with my T-shirt. 'Why are you giving him thanks? He nearly killed me!'

For a long moment the boy says nothing and I wonder if he didn't hear me, or if he just didn't understand. Then he says plainly, 'Wolf give spirit. I give thanks.'

I shake my head. 'Thank *you*, more like,' I say, but he doesn't answer.

I'm about to pass him the spear when I realise I'm only holding half of it.

'Oh no,' I whisper, fingering the splintery wood. 'Your spear! Your spear is broken! I'm so sorry!'

He takes the snapped spear, examines it in the dark. The spear is part of him, really important, and now it's broken. I wait for his rage, for him to yell or cry or thump me. But he doesn't do any of those things. Saying nothing, he limps very slowly to the cave mouth. I suddenly notice that outside the storm has passed. The boy stands there, in the strange amber light, wiping the broken spear's blade on his deerskin.

I hobble after him, my legs feel all wobbly still. Outside the rain is only drizzle now, somewhere a blackbird is singing. My breathing starts to steady itself as I gaze through the leaves of the toppled tree at this Stone Age world that's so ancient but so very new to me: the cloud-rippled sky; the endless forest; the boy. I look sideways at him. He's still got his blue bandage on, even though it's ruched up a bit. This is his home and he knows how to survive in this wild place. Without him I'd be dead. Literally dead. 'You saved me,' I whisper quietly.

He looks at me and does a funny little half-shrug. 'Make safe,' he says, plain as toast, like that's just the way things are. Then he touches his bandaged head. 'You make safe me, Cholliemurrum.' He does his little shrug again.

'Make safe,' I echo back. I guess he's actually right. Without *me*, *he*'d be dead – I saved him too. Maybe now we're even.

Maybe now we're ... friends. From nowhere, a nervous little giggle bubbles up inside me. What would Beaky and Lamont say? My Stone Age friend! I shake my head, half in amusement, half in disbelief. I sense the boy looking at me. I peek at him out of the corner of my eye too and a little tingle zigzags through my bones. Fear? Excitement? Wonder? I don't know.

# HARBY

I rub the ache of my torn shoulder and I shudder, peeking at the dim shape of the dead wolf back there in the shadows. I'm suddenly anxious to leave this cave. Fast.

'Come on,' I say. 'Let's go.'

'Where we go?' asks the boy. His eyes are wide and expectant, as if he thinks I know what I'm doing.

'We go!' I say, trying to sound all decisive and confident, but I can't hold his trusting gaze. I turn away and bend back the branches to squeeze through their net; my mind is whirling. The boy has lost his memory ... so he's relying on me now, but I ... but this ... is the Stone Age ... the Stone Age! How am *I* supposed to get us home through the Stone Age forest?

I hobble out into the golden drizzle. 'Where we go?' I

murmur, under my breath, as I walk towards the Pinnacle, staring uncertainly into the dripping trees, searching for a plan …

But then I realise the boy isn't following me. I squint back through the leaves of the fallen tree; he's gone the opposite way and is shuffling along the stone ledge outside the cave mouth, under where the bridge would be if this was my world. Where's he going? 'Hey, come this way! Follow me!' I call back, checking the forest nervously, thinking of those other howls I heard.

But the boy ignores me; he's stopped shuffling now and is drawing back curtains of creepers, peering beneath them like he's looking for something. Suddenly, the boy cries out.

My heart lurches. 'Are you OK?'

He turns to me and he's smiling, his face all lit up and golden in the strange after-storm light. 'Cholliemurrum!' he calls, gesturing excitedly. 'Look, Cholliemurrum! Look this!'

So I shuffle along the ledge to him and look. Beneath the hanging creepers, there's a shadowy tower of hand-prints – all different sizes. The boy is pressing his own palm to each one in turn, a curious concentration in his eye.

'What're you doing? Is this what you want to show me?'

He looks earnestly into my eyes. His hand is resting on a print that fits it perfectly, like a piece in a puzzle. 'Me,' he says, and he sounds so pleased with himself, I can't help but smile.

'Is that your handprint?'

The boy nods. He looks kind of stunned. 'Me! I member me!'

His memory's coming back! 'Brilliant!' I say, and then I'm so excited I almost wobble off the ledge. If he remembers stuff then maybe he can help me find my way home. I steady myself. 'That's brilliant! Who are you then? What's your name?'

He mumbles something, blinking at me uncertainly.

'What? Pardon? Say it again.'

This time he says his name big and proud, banging his chest with his fist. But I still can't quite catch it.

'Arby?' I try.

A flash of irritation crosses his face. He says the same word once more, even louder this time.

'Harby?' I try again.

The boy bends double, making a puffing sound, like he's choking, like he can't breathe. Alarmed, I reach forward to help him even though I'm not sure how.

Then I realise he's not choking. He's laughing.

'Harrrbeeee?' he says, in a strange squeaky voice. He looks at me sidelong, grinning. 'Haaarrrbeeeeee!'

I smile. I get it!

'*I CHOLLIEMURRUM*,' I say, making my voice all thick and low and chewy just like his real voice, banging my chest, copying him right back.

'I Harrbeeee!' He's really giggling now.

'Hi, Harby,' I say through my own giggles. 'Pleased to meet you!'

He pauses halfway through a funny puffy laugh, his eyebrows furrowed in confusion. '... eat you?' he echoes back.

'No thanks!' I laugh, and he laughs again then too.

'No tanks!' he chortles, like I'm the best joke ever. And his big snort of laughter makes me giggle even more. My sides start to hurt. I lean on the cool rock, looking out, trying to stop laughing.

Even though the rain has stopped, everywhere's still dripping. I breathe a big gulp of fresh-washed air, steadying myself; for a moment it's so quiet I can hear the gurgle of all the little brown rivulets of rainwater trickling down the sheer rock. I peek back at the boy; he peeks at me too and we both erupt into giggles again. I don't think either of us even knows any more what we're laughing about.

But it doesn't matter. 'Come on!' I say, through my giggles. 'Let's get down from here before we fall and break our necks.'

Harby shakes his head, a vague smile still on his lips. 'Who you, Cholliemurrum?' he says, peering at me curiously like I'm a specimen in a museum. 'Why you come here?'

Suddenly I see myself through his eyes. If *I* think *he* looks odd, *he* must think *I* look a thousand times odder! I mean, I've done a whole topic at school on the Stone Age. But he's never even imagined a somebody like me – I glance down at my bloody knee, my muddy trainers, my raggedy blue T-shirt. 'Cholliemurrum,' I murmur in his gravelly voice, and a mad little laugh slips out. I barely recognise myself. 'Why did I come here?' I say to the boy. 'I honestly have no idea.'

He looks utterly confused. 'No eye deer?' he echoes, pointing at the painting of the deer just visible through the cave mouth. I giggle, but then I think about all the other wild creatures in the cave paintings and my laugh pops like a bubble.

I look at Harby. He's suddenly serious; every trace of dancing, twinkling laughter has drained from his eyes, which are staring hard at me.

'What?' I say.

Holding my gaze, he grabs my wrist, tight like an eagle claw.

'Oi!' I say, squirming to take my hand away.

But he ignores me. 'I know why you come here, Cholliemurrum,' he whispers, tickly close in my ear.

'Why?' I blink at him.

He presses my palm to the handprint wall, right on top of the smallest, freshest handprint of them all.

'You come help me find my sister!' says Harby triumphantly, letting go of my hand.

I peel my palm away and gaze at the tiny handprint; something twangs, painful and hollow, deep down inside me.

'Mothga,' I murmur.

Then suddenly my heart flurries. 'Mothga!' I grab Harby's wrist, tight like he grabbed mine. 'Mothga! Yes! Harby, I think you're right! I think I do know where your sister is.' My words come tumbling out, all in a rush.

Harby cocks his head on one side, screws up his eyes, like he hasn't understood.

'Mothga,' I say. 'In there.' I point at the cave depths.

He stares at me, eyebrows raised in stunned surprise. 'Mothga?' he says, shaking his head slowly. 'In wolf kayff?'

'Yes. Mothga in wolf cave. I think I heard her, earlier on, before you saved me.' I rub my sore shoulder. 'Before the wolf came. I'm sure I heard a baby crying, way back in the cave.

'Come,' I say, beckoning Harby to join me. And this time he does follow me as I shuffle back along the ledge, through the net of branches, right up to the mouth of Deadman's Cave. I take a deep breath, then, acting so much braver than I feel, I put one hand on the damp stone wall and step back into the dripping dark.

# DEN

I edge forward through the dark, using the wall to guide me.

I can hear the shuffle of Harby's bare feet on the stony floor behind me. I make out the dim shadow of the dead wolf's body lying slumped in the dark. I sidestep to avoid it, holding my breath and trying not to think about the bloody fur, the sound of the spear snapping as the wolf rolled on to it.

I listen for the mewling cry. Nothing. Just the cave drip-drip-dripping and our own soft breath. A flicker of doubt. Did I really hear a baby? Mr Pasco's voice creeps into my imaginings: '... *somewhat prone to flights of fancy ...*'

'Shut up, Mr Pasco,' I hiss.

117

'Shudda. Misdda. Passka,' whispers Harby from behind me. Solemnly, like these are words in a spell.

I smile, my fear melting a little. 'Shudda. Misdda. Passka,' I say in agreement.

I lead us further and further back into the cave, beyond any daylight, into the deepest dark. Listening hard. Then the pad-pad of Harby's footsteps behind me stops. I stop too.

'Cholliemurrum?' he says. 'Where Mothga?'

And just at that moment I hear it. The tiniest furthest softest squeak. Harby hears it too. We grab each other.

'Mothga?' I whisper.

Harby says nothing but he walks on ahead of me now. We shuffle forward until it feels like we're right in the heart of the cliff. The air is colder here and tastes metallic, like snow. My eyes are finally getting accustomed to the dark and I can make out the dim shapes of stalactites hanging like black icicles from the cave roof.

A little burst of whimpering, slightly louder. We freeze to listen. Echoes make it sound like lots of babies. For a second I let myself imagine that deep in this cave, Dara might be waiting with Mothga too. The noise fades as fast as it came.

'Come,' says Harby; he's moving quicker now. I can

almost taste his hope and urgency in the darkness. I get a little shiver of excitement spiced with fear.

The roof gets lower and we have to hunch over; then we're crawling, squeezing ourselves along what feels like a tunnel. The air is thin, like there's not quite enough of it. I try not to think about all the rock pressing down around me; I concentrate on how badly my knee stings on the gritty floor and the throbbing in my shoulder. Then, I might be imagining it, but up ahead of us, it seems slightly lighter.

At last we wriggle out of the tunnel into another cave, a cavern more like. I look around in amazement. Does anyone back home even know that this is here? Its walls gleam dark blue in the thin light, wet like whaleskin. I look up. It's as tall as a house. Way up high there's a small round hole in the roof and through it I can see a circle of sky. A shaft of thin sunshine falls like a spotlight on to Harby, who's kneeling on the ground, looking at something. And there, in the circle of sunlight, I see ... not a baby ... but a huddle of puppies.

'Oh!' I whisper.

'Not Mothga,' he says glumly.

'Not Mothga,' I agree, kneeling down next to him. 'Sorry, Harby.'

Harby sighs and together we look at the bundle of tiny creatures.

The pups are so young their eyes are still closed. I try to count them as they squirm over each other. I think there are six but they're such a wriggly tangle of heads and tails and paws that it's hard to count. One pup has clambered to the top of the pile and is scrabbling about on everyone else's heads. Beneath her, as if in protest, another pup shifts and she slides backwards off the heap in slow motion. Harby and me both laugh at the same time. With one finger I gently stroke the pup's fluffy head. She opens her tiny mouth towards my hand and makes little sucking noises.

A terrible realisation hits me, deep in my belly. These aren't just pups. These are wolf pups.

'Oh no,' I say with dread. 'Where's their mum?'

Harby looks at me, his black eyes blank.

And I know straight away these are the dead wolf's puppies. The wolf wasn't a he; she was a she. She only attacked me because I was near her den. She attacked me to protect her little pups. It was self-defence.

Gently, gently I scoop up the tumbled wolf pup and snuggle her close. I can feel her heartbeat flickering in my hands.

'I'm so so sorry,' I say in her tiny soft ear.

The pup squirms in my hand, blind and deaf and helpless. Newborn. She reminds me of Dara when he was crying in the hospital, his tummy exposed and his tiny feet pushing and kicking against the air. My eyes fill with tears.

'I'm so sorry,' I whisper. 'We didn't know.'

We've killed the wolf pups' mum. And without her these pups will die. The tears roll down my cheeks.

My pup is asleep, all snuggled into my neck. Maybe Dara might've stopped crying and just cuddled up and gone to sleep in my arms ... if I'd held him close like this. With my baby finger, I stroke the perfect softness at the base of the pup's ears. I breathe her warm smell. I don't want to leave her; I want to keep her forever and love her and look after her; I want to fix the mess we've made of her family.

The other pups are quiet now. Harby has drawn a circle around them with his broken spear and they seem to like it because they've all gone to sleep.

'Make safe,' I say quietly, stroking the soft head of the wolf pup.

Harby looks at me. 'Come!' He nods towards the tunnel.

I give my wolf pup a little kiss and lay her carefully in the circle, back with her brothers and sisters. The warmth of her cools on my shoulder. She wriggles sleepily into her family, finding her comfy spot, until they're all one joined-up bundle. I stare transfixed at the huddle of pups and I imagine my own family all cuddling up together too.

Harby tugs my arm. 'Come, Cholliemurrum, come!' I can hear the impatience in his voice.

But I can't leave. Not just yet. I run my finger gently across my pup's sleepy little head.

Letting go of my arm, Harby limps back to the start of the tunnel; he puffs out a sigh, then he drops to his knees and disappears. I turn away from the pups, my heart heavy, and start to follow him.

A sudden shower of stone and sand from the tunnel opening. Harby comes rushing back in, feet first.

'GO! GO! GO!' he shouts.

He rush-hobbles towards me, eyes wide and wild.

'GO, Cholliemurrum!' He grabs my arm and drags me back towards the wall of the cavern. Jamming his spear between his teeth, he leaps up the wall, grabbing on to a ledge with both hands, feet scrabbling for purchase. Making for the round opening high above us, he hauls himself on to the narrow ledge and yells down at me.

'What? Why?' I say, searching for a handhold on the slippery rock face.

'WUVVVV!' he answers, his mouth full of spear, his eyes full of panic. 'WUVVVVVV!'

'What?' I call up to him. 'I don't understand!'

He stops climbing and takes the spear from his teeth for a second. 'Wolf!' he says. 'GO!'

Then I remember; wolves aren't solitary, are they? They're pack animals. And just at that moment I hear it too: the echoing scurry of wolf claws and wolf voices in the tunnel. The rest of the wolf pack is coming.

# PACK

Adrenalin surges through my body. There's no time to think.

I scrabble to find a foothold, a handhold, but the rock is too smooth, too slippy.

'I can't!' I scream. 'I can't!'

I'm frantic, clawing at the rock. Harby's yelling down at me from his ledge. The wolf pups wake up and yelp like crazy.

I try running and jumping at the wall but again and again my hands and feet slip back off the rock face. I've climbed a hundred trees before but this … this is totally different.

'Cholliemurrum!' Harby stretches his arm down towards me but there's no way I can reach it.

'Help me!' I shout.

I hear the scuffle and clamour of the wolf pack coming along the tunnel.

'Fassssst!' hisses Harby, the spear still clasped in his teeth. He's pointing down, showing me his handhold.

I grab on and haul myself up, clenching my teeth at the pain that burns in my shoulder. My foot finds the tiniest toehold, my toes clench with everything I've got.

'Where next?' I yell, eyes and hands searching for the next handhold.

'Fassst, Cholliemurrum!!' He leans out dangerously from the ledge to show me.

I reach for it, inch higher, but I'm not quick enough. The wolves are nearly here. I can hear their scrabbling feet, their guttural growls, their panting breath.

'Look me!' shouts Harby. 'Fast! Fast!'

I look up. He's extending his arm down to me, shaking his hand like he wants me to take it.

'I can't! I just can't!' I'm glued to the spot; I don't dare move.

There's a soft thud behind me as the first wolf jumps into the cavern.

I hear the clicking sound of claws on stone. I see the fear on Harby's face. The wolf is running at me and I'm not high enough, not at all.

'Jump, Cholliemurrum!'

My eyes lock on to Harby's. I let go of the rock and I jump and I reach and I grasp his outstretched hand. He grabs my wrist. My feet swing out and the wolf leaps up. Reflexively I bring my knees up and they bash painfully into the wall. In a frenzy of snarls, the wolf leaps again.

But Harby's got me; locking my eyes with his, he yells as he heaves me up on to his ledge. The wolf snaps the air and falls back to the cave floor. I lie on my stomach on the narrow ledge. Harby prods me with his foot to get up but I must be in shock because I can't seem to make my limbs move. I peep over the edge: below, the wolf gives up on me and just stands there watching. The rest of the pack has swarmed into the cavern. They nip and scuffle and play-fight. One or two of them sniff at the mewling pups.

'We go, Cholliemurrum,' says Harby, and he helps me stand.

Wordlessly, he guides me upwards. The going gets easier up here and he seems to know exactly where to put his hands and feet. At last we crawl out through the opening and into the calm of the sunny afternoon air.

Harby takes his spear from his mouth, coughing. We roll away from the hole and lie, panting, on the rain-damp moss. Each breath hurts; each heartbeat hurts.

Beneath us, down in the cavern, the wolf howls; the sound spirals and loops out of the darkness, a howl so mournful I feel goose pimples rise across my whole body. Then the wolf falls silent. Utterly silent. Like he's listening.

Somewhere down there another wolf howls. Then a third howl wraps itself around the others, then another and another. Just below us, a wolf pup howls for the very first time, his thin warble mingling with the song of the pack. The first wolf howls again, leading them all. Then, as gradually as the wolves' song rose, it slowly fades away. The wolf pup's voice is the last, like he hasn't yet learned when the song's finished.

'Oooop,' he says, then he too falls silent.

Cautiously, still breathing hard, we lean over the edge of the opening and look back into the den. It is full of wolves. None of them look at us; they're all too busy with each other. They've formed a circle around the pups and they're leaning in, nuzzling and licking the little ones. One of the adult wolves lies down next to the pups and gathers them towards her with her muzzle. Two pups start to feed greedily. Another female lies down and feeds the other pups nearest her. It's amazing; the pups are so little but they just know what to do. One by one the wolves lie down together, paws and ears and tails and bellies and backs and muzzles all mingled until the floor of the den is carpeted with grey fur.

Only one wolf stands alone, on the edge of the pack. He's huge, his fur is dark, one of his ears is torn. That was the wolf who leaped at me, I'm sure of it! He sniffs the air and looks back towards the tunnel, back towards Deadman's Cave and the mother wolf we killed.

I bite my lip. 'I think that one's the alpha,' I whisper.

Harby looks at me, his eyes puzzled.

'That wolf!' he says, pointing down.

Now the wolf is looking up at us, his eyes gleaming dully. Instinctively I duck away but he doesn't seem worried by us or scared or angry. He just watches us watching him, like there's nothing left for him to do.

I think of my own home, my own family, my own pack, and my whole body hurts, inside and out. I feel the searing pain of the claw cuts on my shoulder, the sharp sting of my bleeding knee, and the raw ache right in the pit of my belly. The world blurs as my eyes fill with tears.

I want my mum.

I turn my face away and stare out across the valley: we're on a little rocky platform, so high up we're above the treetops whose leaves glow golden in the sunshine.

Steam rises from the forest in swirling wisps and the air is noisy with birdsong. Right over on the other side of the valley and higher even than us, I can just see the tip of the Spirit Stone, rising out of the trees – kind and familiar amidst all this strangeness. 'Home,' I murmur.

I wipe my eyes and watch some tiny bright green birds that I've never even seen in my world. They swoop and twist joyfully in the air before darting into their nest holes in the cliff just above us. I smile a little smile. Below us in the cavern I hear the shuffling of the wolves. How can somewhere so beautiful be so full of dangers?

As I gaze up at the nests, a cold realisation suddenly clutches my heart. The little platform we're on is about the size of Lamont's trampoline, it juts out from the cliff face like one of those little foldy-down tables you get on a train. I cautiously get to my feet and peer all along the cliff: there's no path down from here; no way up from here either – the cliff is sheer and impassable.

'Harby,' I whisper, my breath catching in my throat.

He looks at me and I can tell from his wide eyes that he's having the same thought.

'Harby, we're stuck! What are we going to do?'

# STUCK

Harby does a very slow blink. Then he opens his eyes and turns his gaze to me. 'We wait,' he says flatly. He looks disappointed and sad.

'What?' I shake my head in confusion. 'What do we wait for? Who's going to come and rescue us?'

'We wait, Cholliemurrum.' He points at the sun. 'We wait. Night come. Wolf go. We go.' He picks up a stone and starts sharpening his spearhead with it.

He makes it all sound so very plain and simple that for a second I don't properly get it. Then I understand: we're trapped up here until the wolf pack leaves their den. Our only way back is the way we came. My stomach churns queasily with dread.

*Scrape scrape scrape* goes Harby's sharpening stone.

I hug my knees and watch a bird of prey circle in the air above the Spirit Stone. I think back to yesterday, when I was there, right there, with Beaky and Lamont, when I threw my pebble up and over the Spirit Stone. It feels almost like I was a different me then or something. 'Charlie Merriam,' I murmur. My real name sounds alien in this fresh wild air.

The sun slips slowly lower. A marmalade cloud like a scribbled Z drifts behind the trees. It must be getting really late. I don't know how long I've been gone, but Mum and Dad will be properly worried by now. I feel small and sorry. I sniff.

Harby sniffs.

We look at each other.

'What's wrong, Harby?'

He has put down his sharpening stone and is twizzling the ends of one of the string bracelets on his arm.

'Mothga?' I say softly.

Harby nods; his spear hand is clenched and his eyes squeezed shut. 'Mothga,' he says, his voice choked and strange like it's wrapped tight in brambles. 'I not find Mothga, Cholliemurrum. I not make safe.' A fat tear escapes and trickles down his cheek. Then another.

I swallow. 'It's OK, Harby.' My own voice is

bramble-strangled too. 'It'll be OK. Don't give up. We'll find your sister. She'll be OK.'

Harby's teary eyes are open now and blackbird bright; he watches me curiously, his head on one side. Quick as a flash he reaches out and touches my cheek. Then licks his finger. 'You cry, Cholliemurrum. Why you cry? Mothga not *your* baby sister.' His eyebrows are low with puzzlement.

I bite my lip. 'I have a baby brother,' I whisper.

'Baby brother!' echoes Harby admiringly, and he pats me on the back, like it's a great achievement. 'What your baby brother name?'

'Dara,' I say softly, not meeting his eyes.

'DaRA!' declares Harby in a warrior voice. Like Dara is bold and tough and brave. Not tiny and weak and ... my eyes fill with fresh tears.

'Why you cry, Cholliemurrum?' asks Harby softly. 'Where DaRA?'

'He's in hospital, having an operation. Because something's wrong with his heart,' I blurt out. My raw voice sounds more angry than I mean it to.

Harby draws back, not understanding, his eyes confused and frightened. He tries again. 'You not make safe DaRA?' he whispers.

He doesn't mean it like an accusation, but that's how it feels. I turn on him, shooting arrows with my eyes. 'No, Harby, I wasn't good and kind like you; I didn't even try to make *my* brother safe; I just took one look at him and ran the other way. And now … it's too late, because here I am … HERE …' I wave my arms in the air, I'm yelling now and Harby's staring, wide-eyed and open-mouthed. '… I'm stuck HERE in the STUPID STONE AGE with YOU and I don't know how to get HOME!'

*Home … home … home.* My word echoes back to me from across the valley like a taunt. A cloud of ragged crows rise like witches' handkerchiefs from a tall tree.

'Home,' murmurs Harby. His voice sounds little and lost.

My silly anger melts and a new lump forms in my throat. 'Do you remember your home, Harby?' I ask him softly.

Harby shakes his head and fiddles with his spear.

I bite my lip. Even though Harby's in his own world, he's just as stuck as I am. 'Sorry,' I whisper.

He shrugs. Maybe they don't have a word for *sorry* in the Stone Age. Maybe when they make mistakes they … do something else to make it better.

'I'll help you, Harby.' I joggle his arm gently. 'When

we get off this stupid ledge, we'll do it together – we'll find Mothga, we'll find your home, we'll make safe.'

Harby stares at me with those eyes that are black and forever-deep, like the unexplored parts of the sea.

'I help you, Cholliemurrum,' he whispers hoarsely, joggling my arm back with his pinchy fingers. 'We find DaRA. We find your home. We make safe.'

'OK,' I say, smiling through my teary eyes. And I hold my hand up for a high five.

But Harby just looks at my hand for a second and then holds his own hand up. 'OK,' he says solemnly.

And it feels like we've made a promise.

'OOOOOWEEEEEEE!' hoots an early owl close by.

'Oooooooowoooooooooo!' comes another owl's answer.

Evening is coming and the light is soft. Harby bends his blue-bandaged head over his spear once more. I lie down on my side and gaze out across the wild glowing valley. We wait. Behind me I can hear the rhythmic *scrape-scrape* sound of Harby beginning to sharpen his spear again.

I squeeze my eyes tight shut and picture Dara in his little fish-tank bed. I wish I'd held him back there in the hospital. I wish I'd given him a big cuddle and told him that everything would be all right. 'Sorry, Dara,' I whisper, and I open my eyes and gaze over at where, in my Mandel Forest, the hospital would be. He could be having his operation right now. 'Make safe, Dara,' I say in my warrior voice, like I'm making *him* a promise too.

I lie and listen to the rhythmic *scrape-scrape, scrape-scrape* of stone sharpening stone. I'm tired … so tired … so so tired …

# HOT

A gentle crackle wakes me. Warmth on my back. The soft grey smell of woodsmoke.

I open my eyes. I'm by a campfire, and for a tiny flicker of a moment I think it's my birthday camping, with Beaky and Lamont and Nero. But it's not. I'm still here lying on the mossy stone platform, high above Harby's wild forest. I've never been up here before, in my world I mean; the cliff's too steep to climb and it's all fenced off anyway, with 'Danger' signs showing pictures of landslides and giant exclamation marks. And I've never been at the top of the cliff before either, that's a street called Windy Hill and it's where all the posh houses are – you have to press a buzzer outside the entrance gates to even get on to Windy Hill. But I'm far far far from gated streets and sensible warning signs.

I blink in wonder. Spread out before me is the endless forest, the trees dim in the lack of light, like they're unfinished somehow, drawn in pencil and not coloured in. On the horizon is a splendid rage of red and pink and gold where the sun once was and elsewhere the sky is streaked in bruise colours: eggy yellow, dark purple. The air is noisy with squawks and squeals and flusters and chirrups as all the forest creatures settle themselves for the night. Well ... maybe not all ...

I hear the skitter and yelp of wolves moving about down there in their cavern den. Soon the wolf pack will leave for the night to prowl and stalk and hunt in the dark. We can go down there then and escape. I shiver at the thought.

I roll over. Harby has made a fire in the lee of the cliff that looms above us. He's crouched down, poking it with a long stick. He smiles a little smile and with his stick he pushes something small and black through the ashes towards me.

While I've been asleep Harby's heaped a little pile of the small black things by my side. They look like rabbit droppings.

'What is it?' I ask.

'Hot!' says Harby.

'I get that, Harby, but what is it?'

'Hot!' He moves his hand towards the flames and pretends to touch them, then pulls back fast, blowing on his fingers theatrically.

'Hot!' he says again, like a warning to a toddler.

I can't help laughing.

'I know fire's hot, Harby!' I point at the little blackened balls by my side. 'What are these?'

'Hot!'

I give up.

Harby has his own little pile of hot black things. I watch him bash one on a rock, peel it, then pop it in his mouth. Even if they are rabbit droppings he seems to find them pretty tasty and I'm so hungry I could eat anything. I pick one up and quickly drop it again.

'Ow!' I say, sucking my finger.

'Hot!' says Harby, smiling smugly.

I find a less-hot burned thing and pick it up. I copy Harby's method, tapping it on a stone until it cracks, then peeling it. The inside is pale yellow and slightly soft. It smells of Christmas. It's a nut. A roasted, toasted hazelnut. I pop it in my mouth. I chew the hazelnut until it is just a paste, letting the smoky sweetness coat my mouth.

I smile at Harby.

'Nut!' I say.

'Hot!' says Harby, in agreement. 'Hot good?'

'Hot good!' I say, unpeeling another and popping it in my mouth. We smile in the firelight, eating and chewing until there are hardly any hots left. We sit together and watch the embers glow as the sky grows dark.

Suddenly Harby tenses. He reaches for his spear. He crawls to the opening, high above the wolf den, and looks down. 'Ttsschik!' says Harby. I'm pretty sure he's swearing. 'We not go yet.'

By his side now, I peer down too. All the adult wolves have gone … except for one. The wolf with the torn ear is lying near the tunnel mouth, his head is on his paws, but he's not sleeping; I can feel his watchful eyes on me. I swallow, rubbing my clawed shoulder.

'OOOOOOOOOOOOWOOOOOOO?' hoots an owl. And I jump.

'Ooooooooooooooweeeeeeeeeeeeeee!' comes the answer.

It's like they're two parts of the same thing. Two cherries on the same stalk. Two numbers added together to give the right answer.

Harby sighs. 'We wait,' he says. I can hear the itch in his voice.

'We wait,' I say with a nod.

I crack open another hot, and chew while I stare across the valley. A few metres in front of us is the dark of the cliff edge. We're so high up it feels like we're in the actual sky and watching the whole world go to sleep. With my finger I trace the route of the river as it twists, gleaming silver in the moonlight, all the way to the far far sea. The sea is so much further away than it is in my world; here there's actually land in places that at home would just be seabed. You could probably even walk all the way to Lathrin Island! Amazing! I can still just make out the Spirit Stone, the highest point for miles around, peeking up through the canopy, silhouetted against the rising moon. 'If we were up there we could see even further …' I say dreamily. 'We could see everything …' An idea jolts through me – maybe from up there I'd be able to see the way home.

'Harby,' I whisper.

He's standing quietly beside me, leaning on his spear. He's got that lost, listening look in his eyes again, concentrating hard, his eyebrows squeezed so close together I can see a deep furrow in the middle of his bandaged forehead.

'What is it, Harby?' I ask. 'Did you hear something?' I

want so much for it to be Mothga. Did he hear her cry? I listen hard. No, just the rustling of breeze through the treetops.

Harby shakes his head, turns his face skyward. I look where he's looking; there are more stars here than I have ever imagined, sprinkled across the sky like silvery freckles. A shooting star fizzles and vanishes ... POW! Just like that!

'I wish ... I wish I could go home,' I whisper, half under my breath.

'... home ...' echoes Harby.

I smile sadly to myself.

Then Harby nudges me sharply in the ribs.

'Oi!' I yelp. 'That hurt!'

'Home!' says Harby again.

I turn to him; there's urgency in his voice.

'Home!' He shakes my arm in excitement. 'I member home!'

# I MEMBER

'Brilliant!' I say, breathless too. 'Maybe that's where she is, Mothga. At your home! That'd make sense, total sense. Well done, Harby!' I leap to my feet. 'That's where we can go! Where is it?' I sweep my arm over the vast moonlit forest. 'Where's home?'

He screws up his face, like he's trying so hard to think, to remember. His big hands open and close, reaching for something that's almost within his grasp. Then he shakes his head crossly. 'No ... I member *home* ... I not member *where* home ...' He bangs his spear on the ground in frustration.

'OK,' I say slowly. 'Well ... maybe I can help ... can you describe it to me ... I might ... you might ...' Hope seeps away again.

Harby stares at me blankly with those ever-dark eyes. 'Home?' he mumbles. Then he suddenly stands taller, like an idea has just struck him. He starts to draw on the rock with his spear, a pale grey line.

I peer over his shoulder as he draws one large dome, with a medium-sized dome balanced on top and then a small dome on top of that. 'Home!' he declares, standing back proudly.

'Home?' I say doubtfully. It looks kind of like a jelly.

Then I look at his picture again, and suddenly I get it. I can see exactly what he's drawn: it's the Spirit Stone, on the top of the mound, at the top of the hill. 'Home!' I say, tapping his picture with my finger and laughing out loud. 'I know exactly where your home is! We call it "home" in my forest too! Look, Harby!' I point across the valley; the massive moon has risen so that it looks like it's balanced right on the topmost tip of the Spirit Stone, like a ball on a circus seal's nose. 'It's the Spirit Stone! Home!'

'Home?' says Harby, squinting into the darkness, not seeing it because he's forgotten it's there.

An idea strikes me then; I think about what Mum always says to Dad when he loses his keys: *retrace your steps*.

Maybe that's what I need to do too: I lost my way over

there, on the Spirit Stone side of the valley, somewhere between Gabriel's Oak and the river … That's where it must be … the portal … or the magic gateway … or whatever manner of craziness took me from my Mandel Forest to this Stone Age one.

A half-formed plan hatches itself in my mind: once we find Harby's home and find Mothga and *make safe*, then I can retrace *my* steps and find *my* home too. I smile to myself; it's all going to be fine.

'This is brilliant, Harby, I've got a plan! Listen: we get back out of Deadman's Cave and I'll know the way to the Spirit Stone from there, no problem. Let's go home!'

'Lego home!' says Harby, as fired up as I am. He grabs his spear and we peer back down into the wolf cavern. The wolf with the torn ear is nowhere to be seen; there's only the grey bundle of tiny wolf pups. We grin at each other: it's time.

Carefully we lower ourselves down over the rim of the cavern. Heart thumping, I scramble with my feet to find a ridge, gripping my fingers so tight they hurt. I get steady then I lower myself again. Harby goes down faster, ahead of me, spear in teeth. I squeeze my toes on to a little ledge and rest my weight and I'm just about to let go of my handhold when the ledge at my feet gives way, crumbling to pebbles which scatter down into the dark cavern below. My toes fumble and flail aimlessly for a foothold on the impossible rock. Then I feel Harby's tight grip on my ankle; he silently guides my foot to where it should be. And he keeps his hold, leading me foot by foot, from ledge to ledge. Until we get low enough for him to let go and leap; I hear him land with a kerrfump on the cavern floor. I'm nearly down too! But suddenly I miss my footing and my feet slip so that I slither down the last of the drop with my bare legs and arms catching painfully on sharp rocks. I land with a thud on the rocky floor. 'Cholliemurrum?' says Harby's concerned voice from the dark.

'I'm fine,' I say, getting dizzily to my feet. My right shoulder throbs and my arms and legs are skinned and bleeding. But we're on level ground now and we're going to find Harby's sister.

We stumble hastily towards the entrance to the tunnel. I know there's no time to stop and stroke the wolf pups, but it's so quiet I can hear their gentle breathing, soft and purr-ish. As I clamber into the tunnel behind Harby, I peek back over my shoulder: I know those pups will be OK. Wolves live in packs. They look after each other; that's how they survive. 'Make safe,' I whisper to the pups. Then I scramble after Harby into the tunnel.

The damp air presses in on me and my mind conjures nightmares out of the deep deep dark. I ruffle imagined poison spiders out of my hair and brush the breath of ghosts from my neck and shifty-stare at something that could be wolf shadow in the thick blackness ahead. I crawl faster, my stomach flipping as fear chases fear chases fear.

Harby is breathing heavily in the tunnel ahead of me. His noises steady my heart because I know at least *he*'s really there. Then I realise his noises aren't just breaths, they're words. Words I taught him by accident. 'Shudda. Missda. Passca,' he chants over and over. I smile, caught for a second between so many worlds. Then I join in too. 'Shudda. Missda. Passca. Shudda. Missda. Passca,' we chant together, and the spell chases the fears away until the tunnel widens and lightens and out we burst into the moon-tinged splendour of Deadman's Cave.

We run to the cave mouth and gasp in big blue gulps of cool night air. Right above my head, a crazy laugh rings out. I nearly jump out of my skin. I peer through the branches of the fallen tree. It's the biggest bird of prey I've ever seen.

'Heeee-hee-hee-hee-hee-hee-hee,' she giggles.

She's gripping a stumpy branch with massive yellow claws.

'Eeeeegill,' says Harby's voice from behind me.

I stare in amazement as the eagle shakes her white-feathered head and pecks under her wing with her hooked yellow beak. I've only ever seen eagles in pictures, never in real life. And never in the wild! We haven't had eagles in *my* Mandel Forest for hundreds, maybe thousands of years.

'Heee-hee-hee-hee,' says the eagle, looking far too ancient and grumpy for such a giggly voice.

I laugh. The eagle gives me a look. I hold her yellow gaze. She opens her huge wings, lets go of the branch and glides low over the silver-gleaming river.

'Wow!' I say as I watch her go. 'Wow! Wow! Wow!'

The eagle perches for a second on the Pinnacle, her white tail feathers spread like a lacy fan on the grey rock. Then she lifts into the air once more, looping back round our way and, just where the water's deepest, she dips down, lifts her talons and snatches a fish straight out of the river.

I gasp.

She made it look as easy as putting fish fingers in a shopping trolley. As I watch she banks away and circles up and up and up towards the moon. 'Heeee-hee-hee-hee-hee,' she calls, sounding slightly smug.

'Fair play,' I say.

I watch her until she vanishes into the night. I turn back to Harby.

But Harby's not watching the eagle. He's staring sadly at those handprints, resting his palm on the one that is his own.

I go back over to him. 'What're you doing, Harby?'

He looks at me with his dark dark eyes.

'My people,' he says softly, smoothing his big hands along the cave wall.

Is he remembering? Are all his memories flooding back?

I look at the handprints and they jog my memory too. I smile – a silly memory. They remind me of a faded old tea towel we still have at home. It was from back when we were at nursery; everybody in the class did a hand-print and the teachers must've got them printed up on to tea towels for the mums and dads. Tiny little handprints to remember us by – mine, Lamont's, Beaky's ...

'My people,' I murmur.

I look at Harby. 'Where are your people now?' I ask.

'Gone,' he says, flat, matter-of-fact.

'Gone? Where?'

'Gone,' he says again. With a deep deep sigh he pushes back the branches and walks out of the cave.

I shiver. I don't understand but I do understand. Poor Harby!

I'm just about to leave the cave after him, when I realise that I've forgotten something. I look back at the dim shape of the wolf we killed. 'I give thanks,' I whisper sadly. And a guilty weight that sits deep in my belly shifts, then lifts a little.

Between the rustling leaves of the fallen tree I can see the river twinkling in the moonlight. I bend back the branches and hurry to catch up with Harby. He's standing still as a statue, just ahead of me. He's making that funny circle telescope shape with his hand again.

I'm just about to call out to him, ask him what he's up to. Then I notice that in his other hand his spear is raised. I freeze.

# SPIRIT SONG

Something moves in the dark undergrowth behind the cave. A stealthy rustle. I think of the wolf, the alpha … My mouth goes dry. Do wolves seek revenge?

Another rustle. From behind me somewhere. The pack?

I look over my shoulder; in the cave, shadows shift and flicker. My heart thuds.

I turn back to Harby. He's just standing there, poised and ready. So still he reminds me of the painted people in the cave. The nearby creature rustles; it's edging forward. I bend slowly and pick up a stick. I try to steady my breathing, imagining myself as Cholliemurrum; a survivor, brave and strong with a spear in my hand. The animal creeps closer still.

Then from somewhere I hear a low humming sound. I screw up my face in confusion; I can't place the noise; what on earth is it? Almost a growl, but no, softer, more like the sound when you're upstairs and someone downstairs is vacuuming. The noise gets louder and I realise that there's actually a kind of music to it; it's ... a song ... or a chant even ... and it's Harby who's singing it.

The animal in the undergrowth stops rustling, like it's standing still to listen. Harby sings louder. I don't understand the words but they seem to be working. 'Sing, Cholliemurrum!' hisses Harby.

So I do. I chant along with Harby, picking up his tune, making my voice low and hummy. The ridiculous thing is that the first song which pops into my head is 'Twinkle, Twinkle, Little Star' so those are the words I'm chanting ... to Harby's ominous tune.

'TWINkle

TWINkle

LITtle

STAR

HOW I

WONder

WHAT you

ARE ...'

I don't even have to get to the *up above the world so high* bit because something surprising happens before then: the rustling creature is actually frightened by our chanting. I see the tiniest glint of its eyes amongst the dark leaves, then it turns tail and runs crashing through the bushes.

Relief floods through me. It sounds even bigger than a wolf. 'What *was* that?' I ask Harby.

'Bear,' says Harby, matter-of-fact.

'Bear!' My eyes nearly pop out of my head. 'A real bear! Did you just scare off a bear by … singing to her?'

'Bear not like spirit songs,' says Harby, like it's the sort of obvious thing that everyone should just know.

I shudder. Without Harby I'd be dead a hundred times over. 'Thanks, Harby,' I whisper.

He looks at me like I'm a total banana. 'Why you give thanks? You make spirit song too, Cholliemurrum!'

I shake my head in utter astonishment. 'I make spirit song too!' I get a little tingle up my spine; maybe I'm learning Harby's ways; maybe I'm learning how to survive.

'Home!' says Harby, urging me forward, and on we go. I walk on following Harby but I sneak a peek back over my shoulder at the place where the bear had been; although I'm so super glad we're safe, a tiny

152

adventuresome little part of me still wishes I could've seen her properly. A bear! An actual bear!

We creep forward, more cautious now, lurking in the shadows at the forest edge, peering up and down the silvery water for predators, but the coast's clear, so we make our way to the stepping stones and we cross. I pause for a moment at the Pinnacle, looking up the hill opposite; even though this forest is so much wilder than my forest, I'm learning that really it's kind of the same. I'm sure I'll know the way to the Spirit Stone, path or no path. Bats flit low over the water, snapping up flies. Just like they do when Dad and me go night fishing. I hop across the rest of the stepping stones while the moon shimmers above me like a fat silver apple.

I hop off the last stepping stone on to the sand and suddenly I realise that Harby is no longer behind me – in fact, he's nowhere to be seen.

'Hey!' I call softly. 'Where are you, Harby?' A big fish flips with a splosh in the dark water.

'Cholliemurrum?' Harby's blue-bandaged head is sticking out from behind the Pinnacle, all lit up by moonlight.

'Oh, sorry, Harby! I couldn't see you for a minute. What're you doing?'

He gives me a look like I'm a total nutball. 'I need

make water,' he says, as if he's speaking to someone very very stupid.

'What?' I say.

He sighs impatiently. 'Take water ...' he says, miming drinking from his cupped hand. 'Make water,' and he mimes going for a wee.

I laugh. 'OK. Fine! I get it!' I say, and I look away, giggling my head off. He goes back behind the Pinnacle and I can hear him laughing his funny puffy laugh.

I scuff my feet along the sand; I can just about make out our old footprints. The boy's barefoot ones and my ones in my trainers. And there are some fresher ones too: bird prints, like little letters in another language. I'm relieved there are no wolf prints, no bear prints either. 'Retrace your steps ... literally,' I mutter to myself as I follow my backwards footprints from the stepping stones back up the river beach to the ridge.

My breath catches.

Another set of human footprints joins up with ours. They're coming from the tangle of reeds and bulrushes, just upstream. Barefoot footprints, but much much bigger than the boy's. I fit my trainer inside one. These footprints are massive.

And they're fresh.

# FOOTPRINTS

My blood runs cold.

Ahead of me I can see the footprints running along-side what's left of mine and Harby's, right up the beach to the ridge and the forest beyond.

I suddenly remember the shadow I saw when we were sheltering from the storm in Deadman's Cave. I picture the shadow person in my mind once more; whoever it was ran fast and strong across this beach. There's someone else in this forest. Maybe it's someone who could help us? I look at my trainer sinking slowly into the huge deep footprint. Or maybe it's not.

My mouth is suddenly dry. I schlupp my trainer out of the footprint, staring nervously into the dark trees. Whoever made those huge footprints might still be up there now, in the darkness, out of sight, watching me from the forest fringe.

Harby comes out from behind the Pinnacle. I watch him in the bright moonlight as he hobbles towards me over the stepping stones, still limping a little from where he hurt his ankle when he fell.

'Come over here, Harby?' I say quietly. I want to show him the footprints, see what he makes of them.

But he's stopped still in his tracks. Wide-eyed and alert, he looks at me; putting his finger to his lips, then to his ear, he points into the trees.

'What is it?' I whisper. 'What can you hear, Harby?' Weirdly, now I'm almost hoping it *is* a wolf or a bear he's heard.

Harby's eyes widen even more.

Then from somewhere in the dim I hear it too, faint but unmistakeably there, it's that eerie call I heard before: the bird that sounds like a baby; the baby that sounds like a bird.

'Mothga!' we say together. We scramble up the ridge and plunge together into the forest, tearing through the vines and creepers as fast as we can in the direction of the cries.

Thorns rip at my clothes and scratch my skin but I charge on through the knotted green, following the sound of the baby's cry. I clamber over a fallen log and into a little patch of dappled silver moonshine.

'Stop!' commands Harby, by my side. I breathe hard; the air is heady with an almost familiar sweetness. Looking around I see where the smell is coming from: there's a weird kind of flower growing here, a bit like the wild honeysuckle that swathes through our forest, but these flowers are all massive and speckled and wrong, like tongue-out faces with wavering tentacles. I lean forward, panting softly in the too-sweet air, listening for Mothga's cry.

Nothing.

'Mothga?' I breathe.

Harby doesn't answer; he's concentrating hard.

I listen too. We're at the foot of a huge pale-trunked tree, I stare up through the net of its branches. This tree's taller than any I've ever seen before in the forest, so much taller than even Gabriel's Oak. My heart pounds. I peer nervously all around us. I imagine faces in the darkness, eyes watching, unseen: wolves, shadow people, bears, babies.

Out of the corner of my eye I see a movement. I spin around, my breath frozen in fear. Then I laugh at myself; it's just a rag snagged on a tree branch, flapping in the breeze like a cartoon ghost in a sheet. Silly. Then I realise it's not just a rag; I walk around the massive tree and untangle Dad's old tartan shirt from the low branch. I stroke it to my cheek: soft as a cuddle after a nightmare.

But … I'm confused … I remember covering Harby up with Dad's shirt when he was lying, unconscious, down on the beach, so … then … how did it get all the way up here?

I hold the shirt out in front of me, as if it could tell me the answer itself. But it's just a shirt – slightly more bloody and muddy than previously – but, ultimately, just a shirt. Could the storm wind have whirled it right up into the forest? I shake my head. Again I think of the shadow I saw. The huge footsteps on the beach. Something shrieks deep in the forest behind me and my heart leaps. I spin around, but there's no one there. Of course there's no one there. Only Harby.

I bite my lip. How did Harby end up where I found him in the first place? All bashed up and drowning in the river? I know he can't remember what happened, but something … something awful must've happened for him to end up that way … I stare at Harby thoughtfully as I bundle the shirt into my backpack.

'Harby,' I say quietly. 'I'm just wondering … Do you have any … any enemies?'

# CAMP

Harby looks at me but I can tell he doesn't understand. 'Mothga quiet,' he says, his voice heavy with disappointment. He does a long sigh. 'We find my home?'

I push the scary thoughts and questions away. *Accidents happen.* That's what Mum always says. Maybe that's all it was, Harby's fall – just an accident.

'Home!' I say purposefully. Trying to force brightness into my voice. 'Let's go!'

But I need to work out where we are first: I feel the angle of the slope, I gauge where the river lies, I look at the position of the moon in the sky; in my world this would be somewhere around the Druid's Well, just down from our rope swing. I totally know my way to the Spirit Stone from here, even in the dark.

'Come on then!' I say to Harby. And I tap the pale tree for luck. 'Make safe,' I whisper under my breath – more of a wish than a promise. With Harby lolloping by my side, I part the bracken and start to run gently up the hill.

We scramble up the little ridge where normally there's our rope swing. In Harby's forest there are vines dangling here instead. I grab one and launch myself out into the moon-dappled dark and back again. I point up the slope. 'This way!'

As I swerve tree trunks and nip under branches and hop over logs, I get a feeling I've had a million times before when I've been playing in *my* Mandel Forest, with Lamont and Beaky. I know exactly where I am and where I'm going; I'm going home. We plough through a patch of mint and the fresh chewing gum smell fills the night air; I laugh as I run through the soft leaves – it's the mint that Nero likes to chew on; the mint that must've always grown here, its roots buried deep.

'Tooth-leaf,' mumbles Harby, putting some in his mouth as he runs.

'Tooth-leaf!' I say, and I chew some too – it's peach-fuzz soft and tastes all green and tingly.

The ground gets steeper as we reach the mound that

surrounds the Spirit Stone. The Spirit Stone that is 'home' in all our games. Panting, we reach the top.

We stand, still hidden amongst the trees, and stare into the little clearing. We're here.

Harby wasn't kidding – the Spirit Stone actually is *home* in his world too: a real home. There's a camp up here, all lit by moonlight: a kind of igloo-shaped tent, and the dull embers of a fire whose smoke mingles with the cloud-wisped, star-speckled sky.

Nothing moves. There's no human sound. Only the breath of the wind in the leaves.

'Home?' I whisper to Harby.

Harby doesn't answer, but he stares at the camp, his face full of searching.

I swallow. 'Come on then, let's have a proper look; I'm sure you'll remember it all in a minute.'

Harby just stares, transfixed, but he follows me as I creep cautiously closer. We keep low to the ground, like invaders, as we edge round the clearing until we reach the Spirit Stone and crouch down behind it. 'Home,' I whisper, laying my palm low on the cool grey rock. A warm breeze rises. I lean into the Spirit Stone and peer out across the endless moonlit forest that is *not* my home at all.

'Harby? Home?' I whisper, giving him a little nudge.

No answer. No cries from Mothga either. Nothing. The camp is ominously still.

The fire crackles and pops, sending a shimmer of sparks into the air. My heart leaps, then I gesture to Harby and we move closer towards the heat and light.

Above the fire is a tall trestle; thin strips of dark meat dangle off it, swaying gently as they cook in the smoke. My empty tummy rumbles. Apart from the tooth-leaf, we haven't eaten for ages; not since Harby's *hots*. I check over my shoulder, then I lean across, snatch a piece of smoky meat, sniff it and stuff it in my mouth. It's so tender I hardly have to chew and it's delicious, like ham would be if ham was less pink and more wild. I grab another strip of meat and give it to Harby – he eats it silently. Closing his eyes to chew.

I watch him nervously. Why has he gone so quiet? Something's not right. I look around the little camp. Maybe *this* is not right? Maybe I've taken Harby to the wrong place entirely, maybe this isn't the place he remembered. I think of the footprints, the shadow … maybe this is somebody else's home.

'Harby?' I say, biting my lip. '*Is* this actually your home?'

162

'Home,' he echoes, nodding, but his voice sounds hollow.

He hangs his head. I look at the smouldering ashes, the little hut, the meat abandoned on the fire. Why is no one here? Why did no one come running out to greet Harby? Why was no one out looking for him? I think of Dad calling Lamont and Beaky, of them promising to search for me in Mandel Forest.

Home isn't home without people, without your family. Then I remember what Harby said in the cave, when we were looking at the handprints: *My people. Gone.* Has Harby's whole tribe really been wiped out? Is he all that's left? My heart aches, imagining how it would be to be truly alone in the world. I touch his arm.

He just stares into the embers. Remembering? Not remembering? Who knows? What can I possibly do to help him?

The animal skins, which cover the hut, flap noisily in the breeze, almost like applause. I look across at the little hut. Maybe Mothga's in there? I try to imagine the tiny baby curled up and cosy, snug beneath a soft deerskin blanket in a little woven crib. I push away the other imagining: a shadow man, waiting in there to ambush me with his flint blade ready.

I try to swallow, but my mouth has gone dry. I pick up a big stick from a pile next to the fire. 'Let's have a look in there,' I say to Harby, but he ignores me totally; he's still staring into the embers, like he's in a trance. Slowly, slowly I take a step towards the hut.

'Eeeeeee-eeeeeee-kurreeeeeee!' shrieks a night creature from the forest. My belly does a flip. I tiptoe closer to the hut.

Gripping my stick tightly, I stand for a second by the hut's entrance and I listen. No sounds, just the hiss and crackle of the fire behind me and my own thudding heart.

I draw back the animal skins in slow motion and peer inside.

# HUT

Velvet dark. I blink; the triangle of moonlight from the hut's opening falls on to a strange lumpen shape. I clasp my mouth, take a staggery step back. It's somebody ... somebody here ... somebody sleeping.

But the shape doesn't move, and as my eyes accustom to the lack of light I peer harder and I realise it's not a person at all, it's just a bundle of what looks like animal skins, all dishevelled, like an unmade bed. I peer into the edges of the hut. There's no one in here. It's empty. Abandoned almost. Like the rest of the camp. A chilly breeze passes; I shiver. This whole place is spooking me out.

I'm just about to let the door flap fall closed when I notice something glinting in a stray shard of moonlight, something small and white and glowy, right in the furthest corner of the hut. I hesitate, squinting into the darkness. What is that?

I step slowly into the hut, the entrance flap closing behind me. Inside, the hut is so dark. I edge towards the moonbeam and the curious little white thing glowing there. I bend and cautiously pick it up; it's very small, it feels … familiar. I examine the thing in the thin strand of moonlight and I gasp.

It's a tooth! 'A deertooth!' I whisper in the dark. A deertooth! Just like my deertooth! The one I found in my Mandel Forest! I pat at my shorts pocket, feeling for the familiar shape of my own deertooth; still there. I shuffle back out of the hut into the moonbrightness, to show Harby what I've found.

He's still just standing there, right where I left him, staring at the smouldering fire. 'Hey!' I say as I approach him. 'Look at this, Harby.'

I hold out the deertooth to him on my palm.

He starts back, as if in fear almost.

'What is it, Harby? What's wrong?"

Then he steadies himself, reaches out his hand and takes the deertooth. He lifts it up to the moonlight and stares at it, wide-eyed. I notice that this deertooth has a little tiny hole in it too, just like the one I found before. I reach towards my pocket to show Harby my deertooth too, but suddenly he grabs my wrist.

'Mothga,' he says breathlessly. 'This Mothga deertooth!'

'Mothga's deertooth?' I repeat. Why would a baby want a deertooth?

His grip tightens. Harby stares at me; I can't read his look. Confused? Angry? Scared? 'Ma,' he whispers. 'Ma make Mothga deertooth. Ma? Where Ma?'

'Ma?' I answer. Now *I'm* confused. 'I thought we were looking for Mothga?'

He drops my wrist and stares all about him wide-eyed; he looks suddenly very very … little … like a lost little boy. 'Where Ma?'

# I NOT MEMBER

'Ma?' I say. 'Is Ma your mum? Do you remember your mum, Harby?'

He blinks down at the deertooth in his hand and his face turns suddenly pale, like he's just seen a ghost. 'Ma,' he says, and he curls his fingers into a fist around Mothga's deertooth, squeezing his eyes tight shut. 'No. I NOT member! NO!'

'Harby,' I say. 'Try to remember! It's important!' My mind starts racing – if Harby can remember where his mum is then surely she'll have Mothga with her. Maybe she'll even help me find my way home! I joggle his arm, my heart trills in excitement. 'Come on, Harby, try!'

But Harby shakes me off and starts that low hummy chanting, like he did to ward off the bear. What did he call it? His spirit song. But this time his spirit song is faster, desperate and feverish. I strain my ears to understand, but I can't; it's almost like he's locked me out.

'Come on, Harby! Retrace your own steps. You were here! Right here.' I stomp hard with my foot. I give his closed fist a little shake. 'If that's Mothga's deertooth in your hand then Mothga was here too, wasn't she. And then? Well? Then what happened? Just remember, at least try to remember. I don't have the answers, Harby; you do!'

Harby's spirit song grows louder. My patience snaps. 'Do you want to remember or don't you?' A sudden wave of anger surges up in me. 'Do you know what you remind me of, Harby? You remind me of a little kid, with his stupid fingers in his ears, going "la-la-la" to block everything out.' I grab his wrists. 'Blocking everything out. Running away. It does nothing. Nothing to help anyone! NOTHING!'

I shake him hard, my face close to his. 'Listen to ME!' I shout. Harby stops chanting and opens his eyes. His eyes that are dark as caves and night sky and bottomless wells. I look into his eyes and see my own face reflected there. I look small and lost. Just like Harby. Suddenly I hear my own words in my mind.

*Running away ... Blocking everything out ... Does nothing to help anyone.* I remember the squeak of my trainers in the hospital corridor. I remember Dara's baby-bird mouth. I remember Beaky's soft sorry touch on my arm. I remember the shriek of the jay and force field of heat and Mum's cry that turned me inside out and I remember running away ... faster than fast down through my forest to the river ...

I drop Harby's wrists; he rubs his skin where I held him too tightly. 'I've done exactly what I'm accusing you of, Harby,' I say quietly. 'You're running away too, aren't you? You're running away from ... something ... What happened here, Harby?' I sweep my arm across the abandoned camp, Harby's abandoned home. 'I think you *can* remember, Harby ... I just don't think that you *want* to remember ... because ... because some things are really ...' I pause, I remember the tubes that went in and out of my poor baby brother as he lay so still and tiny in his little fish-tank bed. '... some things are just ... just too ... too big ... too big to know what to do with ...'

The whole while I've been talking at him he's been narrowing and narrowing his eyes at me. Now his face is all screwed up like he smells a great stink.

'Cholliemurrum!' he growls at me low like a warning.

'I. Not. Member.' His eyes flood up with tears. He turns his back on me and starts to run, clumsy and limping, back down the mound, towards the forest; the moon makes him a long thin shadow.

'Oi! Harby! What? Hey! Where do you think you're going? Hey! Harby!' My voice sounds shrill and pathetic, like a yappy little dog tied to the school gates.

He pauses on the dark forest fringe, glances back at me over his shoulder. 'Go home, Cholliemurrum,' he says. Then he steps amongst the trees and disappears into the dark.

'I bloody saved your life!' I call after him. 'Come back here! Harby! Harby!'

But I hear the sounds of him crashing away from me through the bushes.

I don't understand. 'Wait! Harby! Wait! Please!' I call after him. But it's too late; the forest has fallen silent and Harby has already vanished into the shadows.

I run down through the clearing and into the forest. He can't just … abandon me. We're a team; I was trying to help him; we were helping each oth—

My foot tangles in a briar and I trip. My head clonks forward with a mighty thwack on to a tree branch. For a moment I just stay there on my hands and knees, partly in shock, partly because my eyes have gone all funny. Cautiously, I touch my head; I can feel a bump actually rising under my fingers. It really hurts. I look at my fingers; no blood. I blink, squeeze my smarting eyes shut and open a few times until my vision starts to clear. I can smell mint. Sniffing, still on my hands and knees, I raise my chin and look up. Straight into a pair of huge amber eyes.

# LYNX

The lynx is so close I can smell her warm scent, leafy like autumn. We crouch, frozen in time, face to face, eye to eye. Her nostrils flare slightly as she breathes, breathes in *my* smell. Her fiery eyes bore into mine, dangerously calm, like a deadly staring contest. Her eyes narrow but I blink first.

She opens her black mouth; I can hear the sticky smack of saliva as she shows me her long curved teeth. I draw back from the meaty whiff of her breath. Her eyes stay fixed on mine, and she hisses, powerful and wild and proud.

Slowly, carefully I start to crawl backwards, my eyes fixed on hers. Keeping her head low, she arches her back and her shadow-striped fur stands on end along her bony spine. I see the angry twitch and flick of her tufted ears. I shuffle backwards, scarcely breathing, mouth dry. What do I do?

Then I remember: spirit song.

I make the circle shape with my free hand and I start to chant, low and slow and dangerous.

'TWINkle

TWINkle

LITtle

STAR.

HOW I

WONder ...'

Her golden eyes stay fixed on mine. She lowers herself, shifting her weight back on to her haunches, like Howard Carter does when he's readying to pounce.

Panic pounds in my heart.

'... what you ...' My voice is all weak and wobbly. The spirit song isn't working! I can't get it right on my own! It's not enough ...

'... are ...' I squeak.

The lynx hisses again. I brace myself for her pounce. And then in the rhythm of my own pounding heartbeat I hear the echo of another song. An older song. The oldest song I've ever known. The first song I ever heard, the one Dad sang every bedtime, back when I was little.

I start to hum, swaying slightly. Just how Dad always used to.

The lynx's ears are pricked.

I keep humming, creeping backwards, slowly, slowly.

I lock the lynx's honey-yellow eyes with my eyes and take a deep breath. Then I sing my spirit song. I don't chant like Harby. I sing it. I sing it slow and soft, like a lullaby.

'Row, row, row your boat ...'

The lynx holds her about-to-pounce pose like she's turned to stone.

'Off into the night ...'

My voice wavers slightly, but as I stare into the lynx's eyes my heart fills with an ancient wildness that feels like it's hers, but mine too somehow.

'... and if you meet a wild cat ...

... don't give her a fright ...'

The lynx blinks.

I swallow, then I put my hand over my own strong heart and I sing again.

'Row, row ...'

My spirit song rises into the dark, like it's made of more than me, and as I sing I half hear Dad singing too ... and Mum ... like how when one wolf howls all the wolves howl together, answering each other's call.

'... row your boat,

Off into the night ...'

As I stare into the lynx's eyes, tangled images flash through my mind: Dad and me fishing in our star-sparkled river. Dad's warm safe cuddle. A moth flying moon-bound and white in the dark of night. A birthday wish. A brother.

'... and if you meet a wild lynx ...'

The lynx starts to back away; slow elegant steps, like a dancer. Her movements mirror mine.

It's working! It's working! My spirit song is actually working! I almost laugh in shock and amazement, but I keep singing instead.

'... don't give her a fright ...'

I blink at the lynx through the shadows, holding out a tremulous hand, understanding suddenly. 'I'm frightened of you,' I whisper, dry-mouthed. 'And you're ... you're frightened of me.'

The lynx steals backwards, her bones and muscles rippling beneath her glossy coat. I hum my spirit song. Maybe that's what spirit song is made of – it's not made of words or even of music – it's made of the spirits of us creatures who are brave enough to look each other square in the eye and say *this is me* and *this is you* and *we're both fierce* and *we're both afraid*. Equals. As one.

I sing on, steady and strong; I sing from somewhere deep deep down in me, the place where growls and giggles and unstoppable tears come from.

Suddenly the lynx flattens her body to the ground. I gasp.

A thin whistling noise. I look up. Something thrums through the air just above my head and thonks into a tree behind the lynx.

Instantly, she springs away, her dappled body vanishing into the moon-dimpled undergrowth.

I press myself to the ground. What just happened?

Then I hear feet, human feet, crashing through the forest towards me. It must be Harby, he must've thrown his spear to rescue me again. A flash of anger rears in my belly. I didn't actually need rescuing; I was saving myself quite nicely, thank you very much.

I get to my feet. But when I catch sight of the shadow that's running through the dark forest towards me, I drop instantly back down again. The shadow is strong and fast and absolutely massive; the shadow is NOT one bit like Harby's; the shadow is the shadow I saw in the storm.

# ATTACK

I press myself into the earth, squeeze my eyes tight shut. The *thump-thump* of heavy footfalls vibrates up through my body.

Crazily I think of the frogs that Howard Carter brings into the garden back home, how they sit, still as still on the grass, playing dead even when Howard Carter pats and paws them, until he loses interest and they hop back into the flower bed. But I'm way too scared to play dead. I'm just about to leap up and make a run for it when I realise the pounding feet have gone right past me. I hear a grunt and the rip of the spear being pulled out of the tree trunk. A pause, then the thump of running feet again, snapping branches, swooshing grasses. The sounds fade and are gone.

In a daze, my head spinning, I stagger slowly to my feet. I stare in the direction the footsteps went: downhill, away from the Spirit Stone, curving back round towards the river. I breathe a shaky sigh of relief.

But who was that man throwing his spear at anyway? Was he hunting the lynx ... or me? Somewhere, far away in the forest, a wolf howls. I shudder, looking towards the sound, and notice that the sky over there is brightening slowly. Dawn ... morning ... a new day ...

Then I remember. Harby! No! That shadow man was running in the very direction Harby went off in. I give myself a shake. What am I doing, just standing here? I have to warn Harby! I have to get to him before that man does! I charge in the direction of the river.

Thorns rip my bare legs and tangle my hair, but I tear through them as fast I can. Gasping for breath, I trip into a hollow and as I right myself, I notice something familiar lying next to me.

Heart pounding, I pick it up. My hand fits the smooth indent Harby's hand has made. I touch the splintery broken end, remembering the snapping sound of the wood when Harby saved me from the wolf. I press my thumb gently to the sharp flint tip. 'Spea!' I whisper, gazing all about me. The forest is pale pale blue in the first morning light. Somewhere a blackbird starts to sing. This is Harby's spear ... but where's Harby?

Harby would never just leave his spear behind. His spear is part of him; he needs it for hunting, for protection. 'Make safe,' I murmur. Harby must be close by.

'Harby!' I call softly; that man could be close by too. My eyes dart from tree to tree: What if Harby's been attacked already? Captured? I swallow. Killed? I listen hard, but all I hear is birdsong as the dawn forest wakes itself up. Peering about in the eerie early light, I realise I'm next to that massive pale tree we stopped beside in the night. It's definitely the one, I recognise the branch where Dad's shirt was caught. I edge around the huge tree trunk and I'm in a funny, bare patch of forest, it reminds me of a gap where a wobbly tooth has fallen out. I don't remember this; where are all those gigantic white honeysuckle flowers?

'Harby?' I try again, slowly moving onwards, watching for movement in the trees on the other side of the gap. The air smells earthy and damp like when Mum digs over the veggie patch.

As I part the long grass and step forward, the ground feels kind of crumbly. I glance down and stumble backwards, gasping in horror. I tremble as I cling on to the trunk of the huge pale tree and just stare.

Right where I was about to step there's a big empty … nothing. A deep dark hole.

What is it?

Carefully I edge slightly closer and peer at the huge hole – it's the size of a car. Holding a branch, I lean forward a little to look in; bottomlessly dark. This hole wasn't here earlier, I'm certain of it. Great big massive bottomless holes can't just suddenly open up out of nowhere! Can they?

As I stare in bewilderment I remember something Beaky was telling us a couple of weeks ago about a farmer who was in the paper because one night a big hole, a sink-hole it was called, just appeared in one of his fields. Lamont had heard of sinkholes already, he said they happen some-times when there's been loads of rain, a bit like landslides. I peer into the abyss – this must be a sinkhole!

Then I notice something awful: in the sinkhole, all caught up in some tangly roots, just a few metres down, is something … blue.

I blink and rub my eyes. But I'm not imagining it. I can see it clearly: it's Harby's bandage.

'Harby,' I call desperately into the hole. 'Harby, are you in there?'

No answer.

# SINKHOLE

Harby!

I shuffle away from the edge of the sinkhole, piecing everything together in my mind: Harby was upset, he was crying, he probably wasn't looking where he was running and the sinkhole was so hidden and ...

I blink at Harby's broken spear in my trembling hand; he must've flung his spear aside when he fell.

'Harby!' I call again, my voice just a shaky little bleat. 'I'm going to come down there. I'm going to find you.'

As I get closer to the edge, little sods of earth and pebbles loosen and tumble down into the darkness. I hear them land with a distant splosh far far down. The sound reminds me of ... I suddenly get my bearings, realising where this place is in my Mandel Forest.

'Druid's Well,' I whisper. When we were little we used to drop pennies in here and make wishes – the splosh sounded just the same. But in my world it isn't just a huge gaping deadly pit, they've built a little wall around it and covered the opening with a criss-cross metal grid. So that nobody falls in, I guess. Oh, Harby! I stare into the darkness.

'Harby! I'm coming down!'

I take off Dad's backpack and lay Harby's spear on the ground next to it.

Above the singing treetops the early morning sky is pale apricot, streaked with gold; it shouldn't be so beautiful. I take a big breath and try to listen to the birdsong through the pounding of my heart. A familiar sound rises up from the forest – the call of the bird that sounds like a baby crying.

I freeze.

'Mothga?' I say.

The rising sun flashes in hazy stripes through the trees. Am I imagining it? Wishful thinking …

I stare at Harby's blue bandage in the sinkhole. I inch closer to the edge, calling his name softly.

The cry comes again. Unmistakeably human. I think of Dara in the hospital. His tiny screwed-up face. And I know what I should do. I know what Harby would want me to do. Harby cared more about finding his sister than about anything else at all. 'Make safe!' I whisper. I grab the spear and backpack and run around the sinkhole, down the hill towards Mothga's cries.

Between the trees I can see the river twinkling in the early morning sun. A few steps further and I can see the Pinnacle, huge and grey and solid like it always is. The sight of it calms me, unchanged and unchanging. The cries have stopped. I stand on the ridge, hidden amongst the trees, and I stare downstream, then upstream again; I catch a movement out of the corner of my eye.

A man steps out from behind the Pinnacle.

I drop down into the bracken, my breath catching in my throat. The Shadow Man.

There's that sound again, closer, so much closer, the sound of the baby crying. My heart pangs.

Cautiously I peek out of my hiding place.

The man is huge, dressed in animal skins, his beard long and dark. He's standing waist-deep in the fast-flowing water. In his enormous hands, squirming and crying, is a tiny baby.

I clap my hand to my mouth. 'Mothga,' I breathe.

# MOTHGA

I feel like I'm turned to stone; I can't take my eyes off the man and the baby. Without warning, he throws back his head and roars, a long, wordless sound. The baby screams, tiny naked arms and legs jerking in the man's grasp.

He can't, he mustn't see me but I'm frozen to the spot. The man has fallen silent and he's scanning about him with a kind of fierce intensity, like he's looking for something … or someone. I shuffle lower into the bracken, still watching.

He takes a couple of splashy strides and dumps the baby down on a flat dry boulder. He turns and wades through the river, right towards my hiding place. My heart thuds in my ears but I'm too scared to move and I don't even know if he's seen me. When he reaches the shallows, he stops abruptly, water streaming off his thighs. I hold my breath. Has he seen me? He looks back at the crying baby. I see his hunter's eyes narrow, his hands clench into fists. I'm shaking. What's he going to do? What's he going to do?

And suddenly he's shouting again, and I have to bite down on my knuckles to stop myself screaming. I see spit fly from his mouth. He falls to his knees right there in the river and he shouts and he hits the water and hits the water and hits the water with his huge fists. Splashes leap around him, sparkling in the sunlight, mixing with drops of blood from where his hands are getting cut on the hidden rocks. But he doesn't seem to notice. On the boulder the baby wails and wails, pink legs kicking in the air. *Mothga!*

I want to jump up and scream and run. I remember the thonk of the spear, the heavy thud of running feet, the grunt as he pulled the spear out of the tree. Was he trying to kill me? I think of finding Harby yesterday, almost dead in the river, the gash on his head. What if it wasn't an accident? What if this man tried to kill Harby and kidnapped the baby? What if *that* was what Harby didn't want to remember? I drop down, pressing my face into the scratchy bracken, eyes squeezed closed in terror. If only we could wish things away just by not thinking about them.

Across the river, the poor little baby cries and cries. I clap my hands over my ears. Oh, Mothga. Mothga.

Suddenly the yelling stops. I take my hands off my ears and cautiously peep up. The man is on his feet again, chest heaving, staring over at the baby. He wades noisily towards her, his powerful legs moving effortlessly through the water. The baby cries. My blood turns to ice. What's he going to do?

He reaches the baby. He slides something out of a pouch at his belt. At first I can't make out what it is. Then I can see it and I gasp. It looks like a kind of knife, made of sharpened stone, like Harby's spearhead. The man stands over the baby. The baby wails.

With a swift movement, the man lifts the knife high above his head. I see the streaks of blood mixed with water, running down his arm. The baby's screams pierce my ears.

'No!' I whisper. 'No! Please, not the baby!'

I open my mouth to yell, to scream for him to stop, but terror plugs my throat and no words come. The baby howls harder still. Above Mothga the man holds the knife, his hand shaking. I can't bear to watch.

Then, as if he's had a change of heart, he bends over and plunges his knife into the river. He wipes it on his skins and shoves it back in his belt pouch. I breathe out, slowly, quietly, nearly melting with relief.

Mothga's cries ease to a bleat, as if realising the danger has passed. But my eyes don't leave the knifeman, not for a second. I watch him as he scans the river once more, then grabs the baby, who wails in protest again, and wades across the water towards the Pinnacle. For the first time I notice what looks like a wooden canoe bobbing about in the water; it's tethered with rope to a kind of finger-shaped rock. The man lowers the crying baby into the little boat and out of sight. He stands over the baby in the canoe for a few seconds, staring down, fury-faced, hands on hips.

Then the man strides off, upstream towards Deadman's Cave. I watch him until the trees get in the way and I can't see him any more. As my breathing steadies, I notice the pain in my legs, all cramped from squatting. I stand up carefully, jiggling them to get the blood flowing.

Eyes alert, I lower myself over the ridge and creep towards the stepping stones. Hiding in the reeds where I found Harby's spear, I look over at the wooden canoe; I can't see Mothga but above the rushing of the water, I can just hear her cries.

I don't know what to do. I think of the man, how he roared and beat the river with his fists; how his hand shook as he held the knife above baby Mothga, the blood running down his arm. My body trembles and I start to shiver. He was going to kill that baby, I'm sure of it.

And Harby? I think of the deep dark sinkhole and I stifle a sob. The realisation hits me like a thrown stone: Harby's gone.

But I can't just walk away and leave the baby. What do I do? What do I do?

I picture Harby here on this very beach, in the moon-light just a few hours ago; the look on his face when he heard the baby crying; the way he rushed towards the sound; no thought of anything else.

'Mothga,' I whisper to myself.

Harby had said that word over and over and over; he even said it in his sleep when I pulled him from the river when he was so poorly, as if Mothga mattered to him more than anything. All Harby wanted was to find Mothga, make safe. But now he's gone. I swallow another sob.

I take a deep shuddery breath. My hand tightens on Harby's broken spear; I know what I have to do.

I move shadow-soft and swift, through the reeds. I look upstream, towards the cave. As far as I can see there's no sign of the man. But I need to be quick; he could come back at any time.

The stepping stones are half underwater now but it's still the shallowest place to cross. Keeping low, I step on to the first stone and my trainer fills up with water. The river's freezing after yesterday's rain. A fish flickers silver on the riverbed. The current pushes steadily on my calves.

I reach the Pinnacle and step out of the water on to its lower ridge. The sun is properly up now and the reflections on the river dazzle my eyes. I shield them with my hand and squint upstream.

Then I see the man. He's standing in the river just beyond the cave, around where, in my world, the bridge would be. Slowly, silently, I slip behind the Pinnacle. Heart racing, I press my back into the cold rock. Did he see me?

Carefully I peep out. Now he's bent over a flat rock in the shallows. He's got a fish on the rock and he's gutting it, scooping out its innards and flicking them into the water with his knife.

I edge around the back of the Pinnacle towards the wooden canoe where Mothga lies. There's nothing to hide me when I come out from behind the Pinnacle. If the man looks up he'll see me for sure. My heart pounds.

I need to make myself invisible. Slowly, slowly, keeping

low as I can, I creep over until I'm level with the boat. I peer upriver at the man: he must have more than one fish because he's still busy, scooping and flicking.

I peep over the rim of the boat. Mothga! Her shrill cries go right through me like a siren. I try to breathe quietly, not to frighten her. She's so tiny, a newborn, like Dara. But she's a hundred times louder; her arms and legs are jerking with crying. I raise my head carefully to check the knifeman; his back's still turned but I've got to be quick.

Tucking the spear into my belt hook, I reach down and pick her up. Crouched behind the canoe I cradle her in my arms, how I wish I'd held Dara. 'Mothga,' I whisper, and she stops crying. She looks up into my face with dark dark eyes, like Harby's, like Dara's, like mine. She moves her lips as though she's taking little sucks of milk from the air.

I take a deep breath. It's now or never.

Holding Mothga close, I stand. Just as the knifeman looks up from his gutting. His eyes meet mine. He roars, dropping the fish, and charges through the water towards me.

I clutch Mothga to my chest, scramble across the stepping stones and charge up the beach.

# GLADE

I leap up the bank into the cover of the forest. I've got a good lead but the knifeman's powerful and fast, and *I'm* carrying a baby. I crash through the undergrowth, stumbling, tripping over the brambles but staying on my feet. The knifeman bellows and I know he can't be far behind me. I start to scramble up towards the Spirit Stone but it's too steep with a baby in my arms. I veer right, round the side of the hill, where the slope is gentler and the undergrowth less thick. Behind me I hear the knifeman thrashing through the trees.

Breathing hard, I dart beneath a low branch, leap over a rock and burst through a clump of ferns on to a sort of path, where the undergrowth is flattened. I race along the half-made path, my arms burning with the effort of holding Mothga to my chest. But *she* doesn't seem at all bothered by my running; she's not even crying.

I run into a patch of sunlight; a little glade. And even though I know the knifeman's catching up, I have to stop, just for a second, catch my breath. I step back into the shadow of the trees. Standing still for a moment, heart thundering in my chest, I strain my ears to listen. And I can't quite believe it but the sound of running feet seems to be further off, like it's going away from me. As I listen, the noise fades and fades. I must have lost him by the Spirit Stone.

'I think he's gone the wrong way,' I whisper to Mothga.

Cradling the baby in my arms, I step into the glade. The warmth of the sun on my damp shoulders feels so lovely. I close my eyes and lift my face to the sunlight. A warm breeze passes over my skin, soft as a kiss. Above me leaves flicker and the gentle hum of small creatures makes a yellow sound, like summer. I look down at baby Mothga, still wrapped in the soft animal skin. She's fast asleep. I bring her up to my face and I feel her little breaths, in and out, cool then warm on my cheek. I kiss her soft fuzz of hair. My own breath steadies; my own heart calms.

I stroke Mothga's perfect little fingers. Her tiny hand stretches, finds my own finger and closes around it, tight like a ring. My eyes prickle; I wonder if Dara would've held on to my finger like this. If I'd let him. If I'd held him. I close my eyes and rock the baby gently in my arms, letting myself imagine that this *is* Dara. A warm wave passes through me, soft and golden as morning sunshine. I don't know how long I stand there for, holding Mothga, remembering my brother who I barely even met, but who I already love so much. Mothga wakes. Her perfectly round eyes look trustingly into mine and I feel awful because I realise that Harby loved his sister too and he is gone.

I should've helped Harby. I should've understood. He helped me be brave enough to stand my ground and face all the terrors of this wild place. Mothga squirms in my arms. I remember the little girl in the hospital with the balloon I wanted to pop and suddenly I feel that fizzing heat in my head again, like I felt I would pop too. Maybe if I'd met Harby before Dara was born, I would've been different; maybe I'd have been able to be braver, maybe I wouldn't have run away.

'You shouldn't have run away either, Harby,' I whisper, gazing into the squawking, chirping greenness and wishing I'd helped him, wishing I'd helped my friend to face whatever it was *he* was so afraid of. I hang my head.

'Make safe,' I breathe. Isn't that what Harby wanted more than anything? To make Mothga safe? I feel my shoulders slump with worry. But how can I make this tiny baby safe? I'm only twelve. I don't know how to take care of a baby, not even at home, let alone in the Stone Age.

A cloud passes overhead and the brightness dims. One thing's for certain: we won't be safe here for long. Not with that wild man trying to hunt us down. I've got to think, got to decide what to do.

I wipe my eyes and look around properly. The glade has been formed by a fallen tree. It's a big willow and it looks freshly toppled because it still has its leaves and its tangled roots are dark with damp earth. I walk over to the tree. It's split right through its middle; the split is blackened and smells of woodsmoke. It must have been struck by lightning in the storm. I lay my hand on the tree's smooth bark and turn my face up to the sun. Mothga wriggles and mewls in my other arm. I look down at the hollow left in the earth where the tree roots once were; it's not a deep dark abyss like the sinkhole, more of a shallow crater.

My heart skips a beat.

There's a woman lying asleep in the crater, a woman dressed in animal skins. She is beautiful. Long, dark hair

195

fans out around her head like a halo. Her face is white and she has the tiniest smile on her pale lips. Her hands are clasped together loosely just below her waist. She's wearing a necklace and some string bracelets like Harby's, but they go all the way up her arms. By her right side is a spear, the wood so pale it's almost white. Around the rim of her hollow bed are quartzes, white and pink and grey, and beneath her, her bed is made of petals and leaves and the softest feathers. The woman looks so peaceful as she sleeps there.

Mothga squirms in my arms and my heart lifts. Maybe the lady will help us.

I hear a crack behind me. Before I can even turn round someone grabs my hair. A rough hand clamps over my mouth. I bite down. Hard.

'AAAAAARGH!' the knifeman yells, and loosens his grip.

I wriggle free and dart out of his reach and face him. In my arms Mothga wakes up and starts to wail. The man walks slowly towards us, reaching for his stone knife. I glance down at Mothga, then back at the knifeman. I whimper, my breath coming in short bursts. My eyes dart left and right but there's nowhere for us to go.

Desperately, I reach for Harby's broken spear, trying to

disentangle it from my belt hook. Mothga screams, flailing her limbs about, and I almost drop her. My spear is stuck. I back away from the knifeman towards the hollow, still tugging to free the spear.

'Sssshh, Mothga, don't cry,' I plead, holding her close. 'Please don't cry.'

I've backed right to the edge of the hollow now and the knifeman's almost upon us. Quickly, I step around the hollow, putting it between me and the knifeman. I glance down at the woman. Somehow, in all the chaos, she's still asleep. Then, with a sickening lurch, I realise.

She's not asleep; she's dead.

# KNIFEMAN

At the edge of the crater the knifeman stops. He doesn't seem at all surprised to see a dead woman lying in a hollow beneath a fallen tree.

Suddenly it dawns on me.

'You killed her, didn't you!' I say.

The knifeman stares at me; his eyes are cold and empty.

Just by my feet is a patch of deep moss surrounded by big white flowers, almost like a nest. Without taking my eyes off the knifeman, I kiss Mothga's forehead and lay her down gently on the mossy bed. I loosen the broken spear from my belt and hold it in front of me with both hands.

The knifeman's eyes widen and his breathing quickens as he looks from the spear to my face and back again.

'Not. Your. Spea,' he says, quiet and dangerous.

'No, it's not my spea,' I hiss. 'It's Harby's.'

The knifeman's body jolts like he's had an electric shock.

'It's HAAAAAARRRBYYYYYYY'S!' I yell at the top of my voice, and I leap across the hollow over the dead woman and charge the knifeman, the point of the spear aimed at his belly.

The knifeman catches the shaft of the spear with one hand and yanks it out of my grip. He flings it to the ground and grabs me by the throat. He lowers his face so that it's right next to mine and I can feel his breath on my skin.

'WHERE HARBY?' he yells at me, squeezing so tight I can barely breathe.

The knifeman flings me to the ground. I land on my torn shoulder and pain shoots through me. Coughing, gasping, I rub my throat. I roll over, try to reach Harby's spear, but the knifeman stamps on my hand. I cry out in pain. He gets off my hand and crouches down next to me. His eyes glint.

'Where? Harby?' he says slowly, like he's talking to a small child. 'Where Harby?' he says again, a little louder this time. I see his knuckles turn white as he tightens his grip on his knife.

'Harby's dead! And you … he's dead because of you … because of what you did … it was you he was afraid of … it was you he was running from … you killed him!' I say. I'm trembling all over with fear and fury.

The knifeman stares at me coldly. Quicker than a snake, he grabs my hair and hauls me to my feet. I scream with pain. He snaps my head back and presses the tip of his knife into my throat. My blood pounds in my ears and I feel as if I'm going to pass out. I look up at the blue blue sky. Images flash before my eyes, fast as a flick book: Mum and Dad and Dara. Beaky and Lamont and Nero. Wolf and Bear and Lynx. Harby and Mothga.

'I'm sorry,' I whisper, and close my eyes.

The knifeman's blade presses in.

# WORD

I wait for the blade to pierce my skin, for everything to just stop.

Then I feel the knife tip drop away and the knifeman's grip loosen.

I open my eyes and look up. He's heard something. At the same moment he flings me away from him and I fall, coughing, to the ground.

Then I hear it; a voice, faint and fragile and familiar.

'Cholliemurrum!'

I lift my head up and stare, because stumbling into the glade, cut and bruised and filthy, is Harby. Harby! Harby's alive!

But the knifeman is charging towards him and I try to scream Harby's name, to tell him to run FAST! FAST!

but all that comes out is coughing. I scramble to my feet and grab Harby's broken spear but the knifeman has nearly reached him. And Harby's just standing there, looking at him, not even trying to get away.

'Run, Harby!' I wheeze, but it's too late and I know he'll never outrun the knifeman.

The knifeman grabs Harby roughly by the shoulders. Still Harby doesn't move; he just stands there, looking up at him.

Then Harby says one word that changes everything.

'Pa!'

The knifeman wraps his arms around Harby and hugs him tight.

'Pa!' says Harby again. 'You come home, Pa!' And Harby hugs the knifeman right back with his bruised and bloody arms, his muddy hands gripping tight to the knifeman's skins.

The knifeman says something in a strange, choked voice. He rubs his face into Harby's hair and kisses the top of his head. All I can do is look on in amazement, because the knifeman is … because the knifeman is Harby's dad.

I watch from a distance as Harby's dad examines the gash on his son's head, the bandage gone, lost in the sinkhole.

And even though I can't catch all the words, I know that Harby's telling him what happened by the river yesterday. Harby points over at me; I smile at him and raise my hand in a half-wave.

'Cholliemurrum,' he says to his dad.

Harby's dad looks over at me across the glade. He doesn't smile.

I can't believe it. The knifeman is Harby's dad!

I shake my head and blow out a big puff of air. One more second and that knifeman would've killed me. I know it.

I hear a sad little wail. Mothga. I'd almost forgotten about her. I walk around the hollow and lift her up. She's limp and yellowish; she doesn't look right at all. Her little pink mouth opens, wide as a baby bird's beak, but no sound comes out. I walk over to Harby and his dad.

They stop talking as I approach.

'Mothga,' I say, holding her out to Harby.

'Mothga!' he says, and I put the baby carefully in his filthy arms. He cuddles her close. My heart feels like it might burst with wishing that I'd cuddled Dara when I had the chance.

Harby smiles, his eyes fixed on the baby's face. Then he seems to notice what I noticed, how limp and floppy she looks, and his smile vanishes. 'Mothga sick?' He looks at his dad.

'Mothga not sick,' says the man, shaking his head. 'Mothga hungry.'

Harby and his dad lock eyes, as if they are communicating just by looking at each other.

'Ma not give milk,' whispers Harby. 'Ma in spirit sleep, Pa.' Harby's face crumples, his shoulders shake.

Harby's dad nods and repeats Harby's words. 'Ma in spirit sleep,' says the huge man softly. Then he wraps Harby and Mothga in his big big arms; a tear rolls down his cheek and into Harby's hair.

I stand in the shadows at the edge of the glade and watch while they hold each other and cry, Harby and his dad. Together they walk over to the hollow where the dead woman lies on her bed of flowers and feathers. Harby limps; his dad helps him. Harby sits on the edge of the hollow with Mothga in his arms and lets himself remember, saying nothing, just looking; looking at the woman because she's beautiful, and because she's gone, and because she's his mum.

My eyes fill with tears. She's his mum.

I wonder what happened to her. Maybe ... she just died, maybe the baby was born and something went wrong. I think about how things aren't always what they seem; how bad things can sometimes just happen and there's nothing you can do about it, no matter how hard you try to forget … or how far you run.

As I watch Harby cry for his ma, I cry too. I cry for Harby and I cry for Mothga and I cry for myself too, wishing my own mum was here with me.

# MAKE SAFE

I look up. Harby's dad is coming towards me. I sit tall, sniffing, and wipe my teary cheeks. But he's not coming for me. He strides past me to the edge of the glade. I watch him, hacking his way through the undergrowth, half in awe, half in fear. Even if he is Harby's dad I still don't trust him one bit. I can't unremember the image of him with his stone knife in the river … I can't forget what he so nearly did to poor little Mothga. Why? She's just a tiny baby. Then Harby's dad does something I don't expect. He stoops down and starts gathering flowers: those big white honeysuckle-ish flowers the size of my hand. He straightens up and sees me looking at him.

'Milk flower,' he says gruffly.

He goes back to Harby and Mothga and sits down

with them on the edge of the hollow. I expect him to lay the flowers next to Harby's mum, but he doesn't. One by one he hands them to Harby, who feeds the baby nectar from the flowers. She suckles blossom after blossom until she's had enough, then she sleeps.

'Milk flower,' I whisper in wonder. I wonder how many milk flowers a tiny baby needs in a day … a week … a month. And what about winter? I bite my lip. Harby's dad looks over at me; for a long hard second we hold each other's look.

Then Harby takes something from the little pouch at his waist: it's the deertooth, the one I found in the hut. He shows it to his dad.

'For Mothga, Pa. Ma make deertooth for Mothga,' says Harby.

Harby's pa nods, smiling sadly. He rummages in his own leather pouch, pulls out some twine and cuts it with his stone knife before handing it to Harby.

Harby threads the deertooth on to the twine through its little hole and ties it loosely around his sister's neck. 'Make safe, Mothga,' he says, drawing an invisible circle around the deertooth on the baby's chest.

Harby hands the baby to his pa.

I watch the huge fierce man stroke a gentle circle too.

'Make safe, Mothga,' he echoes. Then he gets up and lays her gently back down on the mossy bed I found for her. As he turns, I notice that he's wearing a deertooth round his neck too, but his looks older, yellower, more scratched and weather-worn. Harby's dad walks back to the hollow and lowers himself carefully down to kneel next to Harby's mum. He lifts the beautiful spear made from moon-pale wood and runs his hand along it, stopping for a moment in the worn-smooth place where Harby's mum must've always held it. When she was alive. He closes his eyes. 'We give thanks,' he says.

'We give thanks,' echoes Harby.

'We give thanks,' I whisper too.

Harby's dad lays the spear next to her, then reaches forward towards her face. I strain my neck to see what he's doing. Harby's ma is wearing a deertooth on her necklace too. Harby's pa lifts her deertooth carefully and presses his thumb to its point.

A bead of blood forms. He draws a line of blood across his forehead and softly draws one on hers.

'Make safe,' he says, and he leans over and kisses her.

Harby climbs down and kneels beside his dad. He pricks his own thumb, draws his own blood lines, kisses his mum.

'Make safe,' he says.

I sit on the grass next to Mothga, stroking her little hand. She holds my finger tightly as she sleeps.

'Make safe,' I whisper too.

I look at Harby and his dad and his mum, all curled up together in the hollow. I think of the wolf pack and how they all slept as one, how they howled together and looked after each other. Like a family would.

Like my family would. My family. Where are they now? Mum in the hospital. Dad in our house. Dara in his little incubator after his operation. Me here. I want to go home. I want to go home and wrap my arms tight around them all. I want to make safe.

'I give thanks,' I whisper to my family, far far away.

Gently, gently I unwrap Mothga's hand from my finger.

The low rhythmic hum of spirit song fills the air as Harby and his dad sing quietly to Harby's mum, taking it in turns. Now and then I can make out some words I know.

'Ma,' they sing, and 'spea', and 'Pa', and 'Mothga'. Like they're singing the story of themselves.

A movement amongst the dappled leaves catches my eye; someone else is watching.

# HARTBOY

At the edge of the glade the leaves shiver and a hart steps out into the glade. He's huge and golden in the sunshine. His magnificent antlers are like the branches of a winter tree. I keep very still.

The hart looks at me. He raises his chin, sniffs the air, flicks his ears.

'I won't hurt you,' I whisper. But I don't think he believes me. He holds my gaze as he stamps his front foot on the ground. At his warning, the forest comes alive with the sound of his herd running away to safety. I glimpse flashes of white tails vanishing into the trees.

The hart watches me until the last of his herd has fled. He blinks, turns tail and leaps away into the shadows.

'Hart,' I whisper. I stand in the huge wildness of this place and just for a moment I let it be mine.

Over in the hollow, I hear Harby sing my name, 'Cholliemurrum.'

'Hartboy,' sings Harby's dad. He reaches out and strokes his son's hair. His eyes are full of love. The spirit song is over.

'Hartboy,' I whisper softly because I know that's who Harby really is. That's his real name: *Hartboy*.

Hartboy turns to me and smiles his small lost smile.

He climbs out of the hollow and we sit together on a branch of the fallen willow tree, swinging our legs. The morning birds sing noisily all around.

'You Hartboy,' I say.

He shrugs.

'I Hartboy.' Then he smiles at me again, a little twinkle in his eye. 'I Harby.'

He looks at me searchingly. 'Who you, Cholliemurrum? Pa says you blue blue spirit. Pa says Ma find you in spirit sleep. Pa says Ma send you here. Ma send you here to make me safe.'

'I'm not a spirit, Harby,' I say, but for a second I almost doubt myself.

'Not spirit!' Harby calls over to his dad. He sounds

211

slightly pleased with himself, like he's won an argument. 'I say to Pa you not spirit,' he whispers to me. 'I say to Pa you not know good spirit song. I say to Pa you not throw good spea.'

'Thanks, Harby!' I say sarcastically.

Harby shrugs.

'Why did he think I was a spirit anyway?'

Harby looks at me like I'm very stupid. Then he shakes his head despairingly and taps me on the chest. 'You not have deertooth, Cholliemurrum!' he says, like it's the most obvious answer of them all.

I tap Harby's chest, laughing. 'What are you on about, Harby? You don't have a deertooth necklace either?'

Harby hangs his head. 'My deertooth gone,' he murmurs. 'My deertooth lost.' He sounds so heartbroken I feel really bad.

'Sorry, Harby,' I say softly. 'What happened?'

He takes a big shaky breath. Then he tells me the story he didn't want to remember.

'Pa go to hunting grounds. Ma big belly. Baby come soon.

I wait with Ma. We wait baby.

Ma face white like moon. Ma need eat boar?

I hunt boar! I climb hazel tree. I wait.

I wait. I wait. I wait. Sleep come. Sleep-story come.

I see *you*, Cholliemurrum!' He prods me in the side with his hard pokey finger.

'I see you in my sleep-story.

I speak your name.'

'I remember,' I whisper with a little smile.

'I fraid you, Cholliemurrum.' Harby has a little sheep-ish smile on his lips.

I nudge him. 'I was afraid of you as well! I ran home as fast as I could!'

Harby's eyes twinkle. '*I* run home fast fast. I need tell ...' His eyes darken, like a cloud passes over his remembering. '... I need tell ... Ma ...'

Harby's voice wobbles. He does a big swallow then continues.

'Night. Ma cry. I wake.

Baby come. Baby come fast fast fast.

Mothga.' He looks across at his baby sister. He sighs and closes his eyes, squeezing them tight shut. I wonder if this is it, if he can't go on remembering. But then Harby speaks again, eyes closed, quiet as a prayer.

'Morning come. Ma sick. Ma lie in forest.

I need make safe.

I not know how make safe.

213

Ma own deertooth not make safe?

I give my deertooth to Ma.

My deertooth strong.

My deertooth only twelve summers old.

"Make safe, Ma," I speak.

Ma not make breath. No breath. No Ma.

Ma in spirit sleep.

I run.

I run down hill.

I run cross river …

fast fast fast …

I fall …'

Harby opens his eyes so suddenly I jump. We stare at each other for a long moment.

'… I wake next to river …' He touches the gash on his head where the blue bandage used to be. '… I wake … I see you, Cholliemurrum …' he whispers.

# DEERTOOTH

My mind swims. I feel sick and dizzy and lost.

The mysteries, all the things I didn't understand, all the whys and hows and maybes, they swirl about like letters in a word search and then, suddenly, they start to make a kind of sense of themselves.

'Harby …' I say, my voice wobbling.

But what can I say? No wonder Harby didn't want to remember what happened to him. No wonder he wanted to forget. No wonder he tried to push it all away.

But you can't just avoid stuff forever, can you? No matter how sad it is.

A beam of sunshine streaks down through the leaves. Two white butterflies spiral each other in its golden light.

Something strikes me – even though Harby's mum

died because Mothga was born he still doesn't blame his sister for that. That amazes me. I look at the baby: Harby's squirmy, wriggly, eyes-closed, fast-breath, tiny little sister. 'Mothga,' I say quietly. But it's not her fault, is it – she's too little for anything to be her fault. She just needs to be looked after. And Harby will look after her. No matter what.

'Dara,' I whisper, and I picture my tiny brother, squirmy and wriggly in his fish-tank bed. Things change, I suppose, things just change and change and keep on changing. And, I sigh, it's nobody's fault at all.

'Harby?' I say, facing him. 'I need to go home."

'Where home, Cholliemurrum?'

'Home? Home is far … far far …' I stop, because in another way my home isn't far at all; it's right here.

'Far far far,' he repeats.

He looks up into the sky. He points up at the pale ghost of moon, still lingering in the blue.

'Home?' he asks, and I can hear the joke in his voice.

Harby does his funny puffy laugh. I elbow him in the ribs.

'Oi, Cholliemurrum!' he says, rubbing his side. He nudges me back.

'Oi, yourself!' I say.

A bird darts out of the trees above us, shrieking; it's a jay. I see the flash of blue as he dips over the hollow where Harby's ma lies and then he vanishes once more.

I stare around me, feeling the angle of the slope, gauging the lie of the land, and I know where I am. I'm not far from home at all: the Spirit Stone is just up there, in the clearing, at the top of the mound. I know where I am.

And I know where this place would be in my Mandel Forest too: the tunnel of trees, where yesterday I slid and I …

'Harby,' I whisper. 'I think I … I think that yesterday … yesterday I found your deertooth.'

He looks puzzled. 'Cholliemurrum? You find my deer-tooth? Where you find my deertooth?'

'Here,' I say quietly. 'Right where you left it.' I look back across at Harby's ma's hollow. My voice fades to a murmur. 'Where it's always been …' Buried deep. I thump the ground.

'Maybe your pa was a bit right after all. Maybe your ma did send me to make you safe.'

Harby just stares at me, his brow furrowed.

I reach into my pocket.

'Open hand,' I say, tapping on Harby's closed fingers. He unfurls them and I draw an invisible circle on his rough-skinned palm. Then softly I lay the deertooth there. He does a little gasp. I fold his fingers around the deertooth and hold his closed fist, tight tight tight.

I don't know the word for goodbye in his language. Maybe there isn't one.

'I give thanks,' says Harby.

'I give thanks,' I say. And I really mean it.

'Make safe,' I whisper, looking into Harby's dark dark eyes.

'Make safe, Cholliemurrum,' he whispers back.

I close my eyes and let go.

# NOW

I feel like I'm rising up, swimming through warm air till I reach the surface and I gasp awake.

My ears pop.

I open my eyes.

I'm standing in the cool green of the tree tunnel, not far from the clearing, at the foot of the mound. Up there through the trees, I see the outline of the Spirit Stone silhouetted against the blue blue sky.

Somewhere a dog barks and close by in the forest a wood pigeon coos.

'Harby?' I say, peering amongst the trees.

But Harby's vanished. Into thin air.

I listen: I can hear the hum of traffic on the ring road. The pulse of music. The distant throb of a plane; I look up at its tiny impossible flying shape.

I'm home! I'm home!

I squeeze my eyes tight shut and open them again.

I'm home; I'm back in my Mandel Forest! The path beneath my feet is gravel and beneath that is mud and rock and deeper still is a hollow and a story so much older than I am. I crouch and lay my palms flat on the ground, remembering the deertooth that lay there long ago and yesterday all at once.

'Chaaaaarlie!'

I freeze.

'Chaaaaaarlie!' Another voice calls my name.

These are voices I know, just up there by the Spirit Stone.

I cup my hands to my mouth.

'Laaaamont! Beeeeeeaky!' I yell.

Nero's bark echoes around the forest.

'Nero!' I shout. 'Neeeeeroooo!'

I run up the mound towards their voices. 'Home,' I say, high-fiving the Spirit Stone.

Nero bounds over, leaps up on me, barking, licking my hands, my arms, my face. 'Good boy, Nero,' I say, rubbing the soft fur behind his ears. 'Good good boy.'

From the other side of the mound, Lamont appears,

then Beaky. They run towards me. 'Charlie ...' says Lamont.

And before he can even finish his sentence, I hug them both as tight as tight. At first they don't hug me back ... but then they do. I don't think we've hugged each other since we were really small. We stop hugging, and laugh and look at each other almost shyly while Nero turns in circles, black and shiny as a seal. He barks and barks, tail wagging so much his whole body wiggles.

'Charlie?' says Beaky quietly. She's staring at me like I have about seventeen heads. 'You look ...' And for the first time in ... ever, Beaky is totally speechless.

I look down at my raggedy, muddy, bloody self. I shrug. 'Cholliemurrum,' I say like it's an explanation, banging my fist softly on my chest.

Lamont and Beaky exchange a look.

'What is wrong with you, Charlie?' asks Lamont.

'And,' Beaky adds, 'where on earth have you been?'

# TOGETHER

'I … I … I've been …' I hesitate. Where have I been? How can I even begin to explain? 'Um … I've been … um here,' I stammer.

'Charlie Merriam, you are officially the worst liar in the world,' declares Beaky, folding her arms.

Lamont sighs. 'Come on, Charlie. Out with it.'

I look from one friend to the other and realise there's no other option but to tell them the truth. So I do. I tell them about the deertooth and about finding Harby in the river; I tell them about the forest that went on forever; the storm and the spea; cave paintings and wolves and spirit songs and wild things; I tell them about the footprints, the camp and the lost baby. All of it.

'… and then I gave Harby his deertooth and I heard

you guys calling my name and … well … you know …' I shrug at them again. '… here I am.'

Beaky and Lamont look at me, mouths open, eyes huge.

'So,' I say, catching my breath. 'That's where I've been.'

'That's where you've been?' echoes Beaky, like the words aren't even in English. She turns to Lamont, widening her eyes. Lamont rubs at his chin.

'Charlie …' pleads Beaky, shaking her head.

'Beaky! It's amazing, isn't it! I've discovered something amazing! Maybe we can find a way to go there again. Together this time. You could meet Harby … you'd actually really get on with him, he's …'

Then I notice Beaky's lip trembling; she looks like she's going to burst into tears.

'Charlie.' Lamont's voice is angry. 'Stop your stupid pretending. This isn't a game, you know.'

It feels like he's just punched me in the gut.

I look from Lamont to Beaky and catch her mouthing the words *Conk cushion?* to him.

My body is trembling. They don't believe me! My best friends in the whole world think I'm just making all this up! Nero whines.

'Thanks a lot,' I say quietly. I turn my face away from them so they can't see my stupid teary eyes.

'Oh, come on, Charlie,' Beaky says gently, joggling my shoulder. 'It's just that you were gone for nearly two hours and ... your dad was all ready to call the police until we said you ...'

'Two hours? What d'you mean two hours?'

'What do you think she means?' says Lamont. 'It's been two hours. One minute you're hiding up a tree spying on us. Next minute, you're acting like a total grumpster and legging it off into the forest. Then, after two hours of us searching every millimetre in this whole forest, there you are running at us out of the bushes ...'

I blink. 'What day is it?' I say slowly.

'I told you it's conk cushion,' hisses Beaky to Lamont, tapping her own head.

Lamont throws his arms in the air. 'Stop messing around, Charlie! What day do you think it is? Same day as it was two hours ago! Saturday! Your birthday, you nutball!'

'My birthday ...' I murmur.

My legs go all wobbly; I lean on the Spirit Stone to keep myself steady. 'But I've ... but I've been ... I've been ...'

'Never mind where you've been, Charlie,' says Lamont. 'We've found you now. But you're in trouble …'

'… BIG trouble,' chimes in Beaky.

'Big trouble,' Lamont agrees. 'Your mum and dad have been worrie—'

I snatch Lamont's wrist. 'Mum! Dad! Where are they?'

'Oi, Charlie. That hurts. Get off!' He yanks his arm away from me and checks his phone. 'Last message says that your dad's going back to your house to look for you and your mum's at the hospital …'

My blood goes cold. The hospital! 'Dara!' I shout.

'We just spoke to your dad a minute ago, Charlie.' Beaky's lips smile but her eyes don't. 'Dara's in having his operation now. Your dad said he'd be fine though.'

The cold, frightened feeling comes rushing back, filling up my belly.

'Dad always says things will be fine,' I say. 'But what if they're not?'

Head spinning, I bite my lip and close my eyes. What about Harby's mum? Sometimes things aren't fine. Sometimes really bad things do just happen. The familiar wave of panic crashes through me and all I want to do is to run away from Dara and all his awful possibilities – Dara might not live and Mum and Dad will be sad forever, or if he does survive he might always stay little and baby-bird weak and then Mum and Dad will be worried forever, and maybe they'll never forgive me anyway for not loving my brother properly right away, how I should, and maybe that *is* actually unforgivable, maybe even Beaky and Lamont will hate me for it, maybe they already do.

My heart pounds louder than thunder. I want to put my hands over my ears and to escape from it all; I want a sinkhole to open and swallow me whole; I want to run run run, fast and far; I just want to run away and forget it all.

But this time I don't run. I don't push the hard thoughts away. I hold my ground. *I member*, curling my hand into a fist, I remember the deertooth I once held there.

'Make safe,' I murmur as I think about wolf-howl and hart-stomp and the family of handprints upon the stone wall. I think about Harby, how he saved me. And how I saved him. My mind fills with the invisible sound of spirit song.

Nero nuzzles my hand. I stroke his soft soft ears.

I'm still afraid. I'm still worried. But I'm not alone.

I open my eyes and look at my friends. *My people.*

'I give thanks,' I whisper. 'Thanks for looking for me. Thanks for finding me. Sorry I ran off on you like that …'

Beaky smiles. 'It's all right. Sorry you're having such a rubbish birthday. Are you OK?'

'I'm good,' I say uncertainly, looking out over my Mandel Forest; so normal, so strange. 'Yep, I'm fine. But … I need to get to the hospital!'

'No, hang on a minute.' Lamont's waving his phone around in the air. 'Your dad said he was heading back to the house to look for you, remember …' He bangs on his phone with his hand crossly. 'And now I can't get a stupid signal to tell him that you're found.'

'Well, I'd better tell him myself then. Come on!'

I zigzag down the mound, Nero at my side. I hear Lamont and Beaky running just behind me.

We run through the tree tunnel, and take the right-hand fork at the Druid's Well. 'That's actually an ancient sinkhole!' I call back over my shoulder.

'You're an ancient sinkhole!' puffs Lamont.

Beaky's laugh rises through the air like birdsong.

We run together up the path and along the high wooden fences; to my gate, to my garden, to home.

I burst in the back door.

'Dad!' I yell.

# MY PEOPLE

The house is silent. Empty.

'He's not here,' I say quietly, stepping back out into the garden.

Beaky's climbed up to peek over the wall. 'His car's not in the drive,' she confirms.

'Probably stuck in traffic,' says Lamont. He's banging on his phone again. 'Stupid message still won't send!'

We slump down together on to the back step. Lamont starts throwing little pebbles, trying to get them into the watering can. My mind whirs. What if Dad got called back to the hospital? What if …

'We know Dara's really sick, Charlie.' Beaky's voice is strangely quiet and unsure. 'You probably don't want to talk about it … I mean … maybe, you don't want *me* to talk about it …'

'It's all right,' I whisper.

Lamont stops throwing pebbles and turns to face me. 'I kind of get it, Charlie. How you feel, I mean. It's really hard when bad things happen. It's easier to run away from stuff, not think about it, and pretend things are all OK …'

I start to feel a tiny bit annoyed with him; he's acting like he thinks he's so old and wise!

Then Lamont's voice goes really quiet. 'Like … like when my dad went away. That's kind of what I did.' He stops talking, throws another pebble instead. His dad left home last year and Lamont doesn't ever talk about him now, so Beaky and me don't ask.

'Maybe it helps and maybe it doesn't, not thinking about stuff. But things don't go away just because you don't think about them.' Lamont's voice catches.

I sit up next to him, but I don't know what to say; I don't think Beaky knows either. Luckily Nero does; he puts his head in Lamont's lap, snuggling in.

Lamont sniffs and strokes Nero's glossy fur.

'Oh, what do I know, Charlie? Do what you like. Think what you want … but I just can't believe all this Stone Age stuff … I want to …'

He faces me again then, and his eyes look older somehow, like dog eyes, ancient and patient and kind.

'... I do want to believe you, Charlie ... but I just ... I just can't. You know?' He shrugs. I shrug back and look away. Harby probably wouldn't have believed in our world either; he wouldn't even have believed in Lamont!

'It's just the way I am, Charlie,' says Lamont.

And when I think about it, he's actually right. Lamont's always been the one with his feet on the ground; he'll play along with Beaky and me but he's never really believed in it the same way. Not like Beaky and me do. Beaky and me, we thought of the names for everything in the forest: 'Deadman's Cave'; 'the Pinnacle'; 'the Druid's Well'; 'the Spirit Stone' ... and Lamont ... Lamont drew the map, and he did it really properly too, on squared paper, working out which way's north and with a scale and all. It took him ages. But he stuck with it until it was exactly how he wanted it. That's just the way he is. He's solid like that, Lamont. I smile at my friend and give him a nudge.

'It's all right, Callan Lamont,' I say. 'I know what you're like.'

'And I know what you're like, Charlie Merriam, you

big nutball,' he says with his old slow smile, nudging me back.

'Oh noooo,' says Beaky. 'You've started two-naming each other. I know what's coming next …' She puts her fingers in her ears.

'What do you mean … Beatrice Bird?' says Lamont, grinning.

'AAAAAARRGHH!' bellows Beaky, collapsing sideways off the back step, like she's been sniped. She hates her real name more than anything.

I giggle, then we all giggle, even Beaky, and Nero starts barking like crazy.

Lamont's phone pings. We all stop giggling right away. Lamont looks at his phone. 'My message must've finally sent. That's from your dad. He says he's glad you're safe and he'll be home soon.'

Beaky winces. 'Sometimes with a message, it's what they *don't* say that counts.' Then she mouths the words. 'So. Much. Trouble.'

But I don't care how much trouble I'm in. All I care about is my little brother, making sure he's OK.

I hear the sound of a car turning into our street. Then the crunch of tyres on gravel.

We stand up. 'Thanks, Lamont. Thanks, Beaky.'

231

Lamont smiles and rolls his eyes. 'Anytime, nutball!'

'Watch out for cavemen!' calls Beaky over her shoulder as they go out the back gate '… And wolves!'

Dad's car door clunks closed. Footsteps on gravel. I go in the back door as he goes in the front.

# DAD

'Charlie! My God, Charlie Merriam! Where have you been?'

He's at one end of the hall and I'm at the other. We look at each other, unspoken questions filling the air. I take a big breath.

'Dad?' I say, a stifled squeak.

'Charlie ...' says Dad, his voice cracking. He clears his throat and tries again. 'Charlie ...'

'Dad!' I rush to him and hug him so tight. He hugs me back even tighter; his shirt buttons dig into my cheek and he feels so warm and soft and Dad-like. I bury my face in him.

'Oh, Charlie,' he says, stroking my hair. I look up at his face.

'Sorry, Dad,' I say at last. 'Sorry I ... Sorry I ran off like that.'

'We were really really worried, Charlie.' His voice sounds small, like he's far away.

'I'm really really sorry.'

Dad sighs and slowly shakes his head. He looks old and tired.

'And where exactly have you been all this time?'

I hesitate for a millisecond. 'Just in the forest,' I whisper. 'I'm sorry, Dad.'

Dad gazes at me, so worried and relieved it makes me look down at my feet and feel ashamed. I can't work out what he's thinking or what he's going to say next. I know what Mum would say if she was here; she'd be giving me a proper telling off. *It's high time you took some responsibility, Charlie Merriam. Try considering other people for a change, not just yourself ...* Dad saying nothing is almost worse than that.

I peep up at him through my hair.

'Dad ...' I begin. 'How's Dara?'

He looks at me. Blinks.

'Dara?' he asks.

I nod.

Dad takes a big breath. I can see he's trying to hold

it together. Trying to be strong.

'Dara …' His voice wobbles. He clears his throat, tries again. 'Charlie, Dara … is very ill. His heart … his heart hasn't developed properly. He's having an operation.'

My own heart thuds. My breath quickens. I swallow. 'When … when will the operation be finished?'

'They don't know …' Dad looks at his watch and sighs. 'They said it'll probably be a while yet. They said Mum was to try to rest and they'd tell us when there was any news.' He looks at me, and his eyes are so frightened I have to look away.

'Can I go and see him, Dad?' My voice quivers. 'When he wakes up I mean … give him a cuddle …'

Just at that moment, Dad's phone buzzes in his pocket. He grabs it immediately. 'It's Mum,' he whispers.

And for a second we both just blink at the phone, buzzing in Dad's hand. We're thinking ahead, frightened and wondering. We know that this phone call will change everything.

'Hello,' says Dad. He goes into the living room and closes the door.

# NEWS

I run upstairs and lie on my bed cuddling Howard Carter. He purrs and nudges my hand with his chin every time I stop stroking him. I look into his eyes and think of the lynx. I thump the rhythm of my spirit song softly on my pillow. My window's open and outside I can hear the trees of Mandel Forest whispering gently in the breeze.

After what feels like about a hundred years I hear Dad's slow footsteps on the stairs. I leap to my feet. Dad puts his head around my door.

'Dad,' I say, my voice all squeaky. 'Tell me about Dara. Is Dara OK?' Dad puts his hands on my shoulders. He looks me straight in the eye.

'Dara ...' he says, speaking my brother's name in the

wispy way. His breath catches in his throat and he swallows hard.

I feel like I'm falling from the tallest tree, like I'm diving to the depths of a well. Down down down. My whole body tenses as I wait for the crash and the splash and the snap and the break of my own ending.

'DaRA!' I say his name how Harby said it, like he's a warrior, like I'm a warrior too. 'DARA!'

'Charlie,' says Dad. He's shaking his head, over and over; tears stream down his cheeks. Then I notice that he's smiling too. 'It went OK, Charlie,' Dad squeaks. 'Dara's operation went OK.'

Relief surges through me. My eyes fill up with tears. Dad pulls me close and hugs me tight. I wrap my arms around him and soak his shirt with my tears. I can feel the gasp and shudder of his sobs.

'So,' I say into his chest, my voice all muffled. 'If it's good news, then why are we crying?'

'Dunno,' he says, pulling one arm away to blow his nose, 'must be the onions.'

I laugh through my own tears.

'Dad, there are no stupid onions.' I grab a tissue and blow my nose too. 'It's OK to cry, you know. Even cavemen cry.'

'That is such a Charlie Merriam thing to say.' He kisses the top of my head. 'You stink of dog.'

'Nero,' I say, by way of explanation.

Dad shrugs; he doesn't see me shiver, remembering the wolf.

Then Dad does a double take. 'Charlie!' he gasps. 'Would you just look at the state of you!'

Dad takes my shoulders again and holds me at arm's length. 'What on earth have you been up to? You're covered in cuts, Charlie! And you're absolutely filthy; I'll run you a bath, love.'

'No, Dad. Let's go to the hospital right now! I want to see Dara. I want to see Mum.'

'Catch yourself on, Charlie.' Dad's eyebrows almost hit the ceiling. 'Do you really want to see Mum looking like that? She'd have a fit. In fact they probably wouldn't even let you into the hospital – you're a walking health hazard!'

I smile, but then I notice that, even though Dad's joking around like normal, his eyes aren't smiling. Coldness creeps into my blood once more.

'Dad,' I say softly. 'You've told me the good news. But is there any …' I swallow. '… any bad news?'

'Oh, the bad news?' Dad blinks, hesitating. 'The bad

news is that little brothers are really annoying. You'll come to realise this, Charlie; they break all your stuff, thump you and they eat a lot.'

I smile weakly. 'Seriously, Dad, tell me the real bad news. I want to know.'

# PROMISE

Dad looks at me long and hard, like he's seeing me for the first time. He sighs.

'It's not going to be easy, Charlie. Dara's still in intensive care and he's going to be in hospital for a while. He may have problems with his heart his whole life. He'll need more operations when he's bigger. And Mum ...' Dad's voice trails away.

He picks up the photo on my bedside table – the three of us, when I was just born. I look at it too; Dad's grinning really goofily and Mum's laughing, cuddling me tight.

Real Dad, now Dad, sighs. 'Our lives are going to be a bit different, Charlie. Mum's really shaken up. We all are.' Dad's talking to me properly. Like I'm a grown-up. Like we're in this together.

'Maybe we're all a little bit different, Dad,' I say quietly. 'And a bit the same. Things happen, bad things sometimes, and sometimes people get a bit broken, don't they?' Dad nods. 'But we'll look after each other, won't we? That's what we do.'

I look into Dad's eyes; he understands.

Dad reaches out and strokes my hair. He pulls out a bit of twig and raises his eyebrows at me. 'Wild thing!' he says. 'I'll go and run you that bath.'

'I'll have a shower,' I say. 'Then let's go and see Mum and Dara.'

'OK,' says Dad. 'Dara's got a birthday present waiting in the hospital for you actually.'

I laugh.

Dad trots downstairs. 'What do you want for lunch, Charlie?'

'Everything!' I call back down.

Standing beneath the steaming water, I watch the mud and leaves and blood swirl down the plughole. The past doesn't all wash away that easily; some things get lost or forgotten or left behind, but they're always there, buried deep, waiting to be found. Just like I found Harby's deer-tooth. With my finger I draw an invisible circle on my throat, right where a make-safe-deertooth would lie. But

241

maybe it's not just a deertooth that makes safe, maybe it's people, maybe it's us.

In my room, I put on a fresh T-shirt, another blue one. I hear a blackbird calling from outside my open window. I kneel on my bed and look out over the garden into Mandel Forest. A wood pigeon perches on the flickering beech tree; his feathers are the colours of early morning sky, grey and pink and silver.

'Whhhooooo?' he calls.

'Charlie Merriam,' I answer.

'Whhhooooooo?' he asks again.

And I whisper, Cholliemurrum.

Because I am both.

The warm smells of lunch rise up the stairs. I pick up the photo of us from twelve years ago. Today we'll take another photo, of all of us together, our family; we'll be different but still really the same. In today's photo, I'll be the one cuddling the tiny, newborn baby, I'll have a goofy grin on my face and a heart full of love. And when I hold my little brother, Dara Merriam, for the very first time, I'll make him a promise, the same promise that Harby made to Mothga, right here, so very very long ago.

*Make safe*, I'll whisper in Dara's little ear. And I will.

THE END

# I GIVE THANKS ...

... To everyone at Bloomsbury Children's – I am so lucky to have found my (wild way) home with you. To Lucy Mackay-Sim, my kind-hearted, clever, creative editor, you have given so much to me and to this book – I love working with you. To wonderful Ellen Holgate, thank you for saying YES and for asking me the questions I needed to ask my story. Also to Jessica Bellman, Michael Young, Bea Cross, Jade Westwood, Jess White, Sarah Taylor-Fergusson, the Rights team, the Sales team and all at Bloomsbury Australia too.

... To Ben Mantle for this cover that just glimmers with adventure and shivers with danger too. To Patrick Knowles for the exquisite hand lettering and to Sarah Baldwin for weaving it all together so enchantingly.

... To Nancy Miles, my utterly marvellous agent. You have guided me ... and Charlie ... so clear-sightedly through this forest. We'd be lost without you!

... To the flock, the herd, the shoal that is the MA in Writing for Young People at Bath Spa University – I am proud and grateful to swim, run and fly alongside you all. My particular love and thanks to Julia Green who nurtured and nourished the heart of this book and to Steve Voake who first shook Hartboy's voice awake. Also to David Almond, C. J. Skuse, Lucy Christopher, Jo Nadin and Claire Furniss. And, of course, to my dear workshop pals. Thank you, all of you, for caring for this story so gently and wisely when it was newly hatched.

... To my treasured tribes of writing friends – Aubergines, Stroops, Swaggers, Scoobies. Most especially Hana Tooke, Nizrana Farook, Lucy Cuthew, Yasmin Rahman, Rachel Huxley and Sue Bailey – thank you for reading my words so thoughtfully and for writing your own words so inspiringly. I'm proud to have such talented, kind, supportive (and ever-so-slightly mischievous) friends.

*The Wild Way Home* is about the shared adventure of friendship and this story is interwoven with wisps of all the amazing *real* people I've been so lucky to adventure with. Thank you, all my friends, for sharing your wild ways with me; I hope you each spy your influence in this book. Particularly big bear hugs to Emma, Laura, Zuri, Corinne, Aynsley, Cath, Tanya, Clairey, Hannah, Jo and Claire.

As Charlie and Hartboy could tell us, home is family. Thank you to all my Kirtley family for your love, support and encouragement, especially Sylvia and Peter. Thank you to my Logan family for a lifetime of blethering, dandering and general ligging around; Dad, Anna, Alice and Niall, this story has deep roots in you. To Amy, who has shared everything and who remembers my own memories better than I ever do. To dearest Dorrie. And of course to Mum – who has given me so so much and who is, quite simply, my hero.

Most of all I give thanks to my very own wolf pack: to my cubs, Lyla, Arlo and Flora, and to Andrew, my mate-for-life. You are everything: you inspire me; you question me; you make me laugh; you make me think. You've given me time and space to become an actual author, and you've believed in this story (and in me) from the start. I want to howl from the hilltops how very much I love you all.

This story is wrapped in pre-history; I owe a great debt to the late Professor Peter Woodman – the archaeologist who excavated the Mesolithic site at Mount Sandel in Northern Ireland. That place, where I played when I was a wee girl, is what inspired this story. As did the real Stone Age people, whose long-lost footprints we all walk upon every single day. I give thanks especially to them – our Stone Age ancestors; I'm sure they dreamed and wished and laughed and loved and wept and hoped just as much as we all still do.

And finally, dear readers, thank *you*; without you this story would only be pages on a shelf or whispers in the wind.

Be kind. Have adventures. Make safe.